THE GILDED DISCIPLE

MITCH HERRON 8

STEVE P. VINCENT

The Gilded Disciple © 2023 Steve P. Vincent

1

———————

Somewhere in the suburbs north of Washington D.C. stood a quiet home on a neatly landscaped lot, surrounded by tall trees and a lush green lawn. The house had a warm, inviting facade and a wraparound porch. The lights were on, and a reasonably new Toyota in the driveway suggested the occupants were home.

It could be a postcard illustration of The American Dream.

Mitch Herron knew little of that. Dressed all in black and with a pistol stuffed into the waistband of his pants, he leaned against a tree, careful to stay away from the light bleeding from the house's windows. He could only imagine what the family inside did to fill their day; not since he was a small child had he enjoyed something so mundane as eating and sleeping in one place for more than a few weeks.

The house was home to the family of a Chinese businessman named Sheng Yu, who'd lived and worked in the United States for several decades. He'd made his fortune in the import business, politically connected enough in both countries to skirt around any friction in the relationship between the two nations.

But his influence had extended beyond that.

He'd been a double agent, working for both the Chinese and American governments.

Only days ago, Herron had fought to hell and back to find him, a last-ditch effort to foil China's impending invasion of Taiwan. Sheng – using his influence – had brought the invasion to a screeching halt, but at the cost of revealing his treason. He'd been tortured and wounded, and now he and his family were the target of a vengeful government that had seen its most important strategic aim foiled.

To secure his cooperation and end the invasion, Herron had promised to protect Sheng's family until he could receive medical care and return home. Once he was home, Sheng could pack them up and go into hiding, but until then, they would have a guardian hiding in the shadows.

Herron had been at it for days, watching the house from inside a car he'd stolen in the daylight hours, before moving closer to the house after dark. It was a miracle the Chinese Government's goons hadn't already shown up, and Herron was hoping Sheng would soon return to take his family to safety. Then he could hit the road.

His priority would be finding Erica Kearns and telling her she could come out of hiding.

The scientist who'd once helped him eradicate the Omega Strain, Kearns meant a lot to Herron and had sacrificed a lot for him. She'd been forced into hiding a second time after the American Director of National

Intelligence had threatened her safety, coercing Herron into helping to stop the invasion of Taiwan. Now the incursion had been stopped and the DNI had been killed, there was no reason for her to stay hidden.

But once again, Sheng hadn't shown today. And once again, Herron would wait in the darkness until the family went to bed, then return to his car to eat and get a few hours of sleep, hopeful tomorrow would be the day he could hit the road to find Kearns.

He settled back into waiting, the minutes and hours passing like nothing to him. In his career, he'd spent days lying in cold mud, looking down the scope of a sniper rifle, waiting for the perfect shot. He'd hidden in a broom closet for a day, waiting for a target to return home before springing out to garrotte him. He'd done all that and more, dozens of kills and missions in far more trying conditions than this.

In comparison, hanging outside a suburban house while dry and warm enough was easy.

On the other side of the lawn, a stick cracked.

Herron drew his pistol, his eyes probing the darkness for any sign of an intruder. Simultaneously, his ears went to work, trying to locate another sound source that might give a hint about what he was facing and where. He detected nothing, but despite that, there was a good chance something or someone had entered the yard.

He inched closer to the house, crossing the well-manicured lawn as quiet as a whisper. He was careful to avoid any source of light, lest he be seen by a neighbor or passing car – or a hit team – although he wasn't concerned that the people inside the house might spot him. With all the lights on, the home's occupants would have crappy night vision, so if they looked out the window they'd see nothing but darkness.

He slipped from the eastern side of the house to the west – a full sweep of the front. He was beginning to wonder if the sound had been caused by a passing animal when he heard the rustle of leaves from the backyard.

With less concern for stealth now, Herron took fast strides to the fence at the side of the house. It stood about shoulder-height and divided the front yard and the back. And, having established days ago the family didn't have a dog to give away his presence, Herron leapt up and over it in one powerful movement.

Dropping silently to the ground, he swung his pistol in an arc, searching for a target.

He expected to find a Chinese hit team or solo asset.

Instead, he saw nothing.

Frowning, Herron moved across the yard, his senses working overtime as he skillfully negotiated the clutter littering the ground: children's toys, potted plants, and other detritus that showed a space was both loved and lived in. He continued through the yard, past the back of the house, until he reached the twin of the fence he'd just jumped, which separated the other side of the building from the front.

Again, he found nothing.

His next priority was to make sure nobody was already in the house who shouldn't be. Looping back to the rear of the house, he peered inside the window. Sheng's wife was seated at the head of a dining table, her two young children perched on either side of her, eagerly eating their dinner. Steam rose from the food that filled their plates, and the children chattered excitedly. While Herron couldn't hear a word, the smiles around the table told him everything was okay.

Strangely, the family didn't seem bothered by the absence of their father. Herron could only explain this by the fact that Sheng's work would likely take him abroad often. Whether he was right or wrong, the family meal looked like a moment of calm and togetherness, one that the mother and her children would always cherish.

One Herron would never know.

Deciding that whatever had made the noises wasn't a threat, Herron retraced his steps, climbing back over the fence towards the front of the house, putting his pistol away along the way. Soon enough, he was back in his original perch, ready to watch the house for a few more hours yet. At least until a few moments later, headlights cut a bright beam down the street, and a car pulled to a stop outside the house.

Herron used the tree trunk to shield himself from the car and its occupants. "Keep on driving down the street, asshole."

One of the car doors opened and then closed, the sound like a cannon shot on the otherwise deathly quiet street. A second later, Herron heard the clop-clop-clop of heavy boots on the sidewalk, before the car pulled away and continued up the street. Silently, he drew his pistol again, then rounded the tree and raised it. This time he didn't have to work very hard to find a target, aiming squarely at the new arrival.

The man, who was walking with a heavy limp, came to an abrupt halt.

"Easy, pal," Herron said, his voice loud enough to be heard by the man but nobody else – especially not the family eating dinner at the back of the house. "Stop where you are."

The mystery figure complied, then spoke. "It's me. I've come to see my family and get them to safety."

Sheng.

Herron lowered the pistol and smiled. "Took your damn time."

"I had to spend longer in the hospital than I'd hoped."

"No kidding," Herron said, taking in the sight of Sheng's face, which was still a mess of cuts and bruises. Herron stuffed the pistol back into his waistband. "You did good."

"And you made sure my family here didn't pay the price for it." Sheng held out a hand. "Thank you."

Herron shook Sheng's hand. "I'll stick around outside while you pack your family up, then hit the road."

"Let me at least offer you a hot meal and a warm shower while you wait, then we can leave together."

Herron considered the offer, then nodded. "Okay. Where are you planning to go?"

"To a friend's house. From there, I'm not sure, but we have money and contacts, so we'll be okay."

Herron followed Sheng to the front door, staying back a little while he knocked. Eventually, Sheng's wife opened the door, a look of suspicion on her face – it wasn't normal to have visitors at this hour. A second later, her expression became one of relief at seeing her husband, flashing to concern when she noticed his injuries. Despite this, she didn't ask questions, hinting she may know her husband's *other* role.

As she stepped forward and embraced Sheng, her

eyes glanced at Herron. Waiting patiently until they were done, he stepped forward and held out his hand. "I'm... Kevin."

She shook his hand. "Do you work with the business?"

"Something like that. Nice to meet you."

She nodded. "Come inside, both of you. There's some food left from dinner if you're hungry."

They made their way through the house until they reached the dining room, Herron staying back a little as the children boisterously greeted their father. Sheng's daughter – who looked to be the younger of the children – blinked a few times, leapt from her seat at the dining table, and ran to embrace her dad. She barely came up to his waist, so she hugged his leg while Sheng ruffled her hair. Sheng's son also wrapped his arms around his father.

"Good to see you, kids," Sheng said, wincing as his son squeezed a little too hard, aggravating some wound under his clothing. "Now sit down. Eat."

Slowly, the children disengaged and returned to the table, smiles still lighting up their faces. Their mother heaped their plates high once again, then did the same for Sheng and Herron, who sat at two empty spaces. They settled into easy conversation, Herron simply listening as he ate. The two topics he'd expected to come up – who he was and where Sheng had been for several days – were left unaddressed. Sheng's wife clearly knew to keep quiet about such matters.

When they'd all had their fill, Sheng's wife excused the children, then pulled out a bottle of some sort of clear liquor. Herron assumed it was some sort of Chinese spirit, accepting the glass she poured for him and downing it in one shot. It burned like fire for a second, but he enjoyed it well enough.

"Another?" Sheng held up the bottle, half-tilting it as if ready to pour. "For luck?"

"My luck hasn't failed me yet," Herron said. "But too many more of those and it might."

"Okay," Sheng replied and put the bottle on the table. "I'll show you to the shower."

Herron nodded and stood. After thanking Sheng's wife for the meal, he started back through the house, Sheng following but making no further small talk. Yet when Herron passed a window, getting his first look outside in a while, he froze, his mind shouting a warning as loud as a sonic boom.

There was a van parked out front.

Herron couldn't be sure anything was amiss, but the van hadn't been parked there before, nor had it been there at any other time during the few days he'd been keeping watch. It was some coincidence that it had arrived in the dead of night on the otherwise quiet street and parked right out front of the house just after the injured Sheng returned home.

And Herron didn't believe in coincidences.

He shoved Sheng back toward the dining room, then drew his pistol. "Don't ask questions, just get your family to the center of the house and away from the windows, and hide if possible."

Sheng's footsteps pounded through the house as he rushed back to his wife and children. Herron swiftly appraised the living room around him, his eyes settling on a heavy coffee table. He turned it over and took cover behind it; his position gave him a good view of the front door, which he covered with his pistol. If the van held operatives, it wouldn't be long before they breached the building.

Sure enough, a second later, the front door burst open, and several helmeted men poured into the room, submachine guns raised. Herron fired instantly, his razor-sharp senses giving him the initiative. He planted his first and second shots right on target, hitting the first attacker in the small gap between his helmet and his body armor. Shifting aim, he did the same to the second. Both dropped.

But Herron wasn't about to wait for more attackers to spring through the door. He'd used the element of surprise to his advantage, but with that spent, he was outnumbered, outgunned, and out positioned. If the team was worth their salt, they'd be entering through multiple points – likely the front and back doors, and possibly some windows as well.

Winning here wasn't enough.

He kept as low as possible as he burst from cover, heading back through the house to find Sheng and his family. Behind him, an operative cursed as he tripped over his fallen comrades, buying Herron the precious second he needed to avoid being filled with lead.

It took a second to realize the man had spoken English.

With an American accent.

Lacking the time to process the ramifications of this, Herron bounded down the hallway, stealth replaced by urgency. Bursting into the dining room where, only moments ago, he'd been enjoying a home-cooked meal, Herron intercepted two operatives who'd come in through the back door. The pair weren't surprised, so his arrival was met with gunfire.

Sliding like a baseball player desperate to reach home, Herron threw himself beneath their opening burst of fire and under the dining table. Before he'd even stopped moving, he unloaded his remaining ammo into the feet and shins of one operative. While the intruders' heads and upper bodies were well protected by their armor, their lower halves were a different story, and the man fell, screaming and out of the fight for now.

Herron used his momentum to shift his slide to a roll, coming to a stop at the feet of the second gunman. As the man's gun lowered to shoot him, Herron gripped the barrel, using it to pull himself up, while keeping the thing pointed away from him. The operative kicked out, and Herron grunted as one blow connected with his torso, still bruised from the injuries he received days before.

Up on his feet, and still corralling the gun, Herron pistol-whipped the operative. The impact landed over where the intruder's ear should be inside the helmet, stunning him. Simultaneously, with his free hand, Herron let go of the barrel of the submachine gun, instead slipping his thumb inside the trigger guard. Using all his strength, he forced the weapon up, and when it was in position, he jammed his thumb down on the trigger.

The operative's head jerked back as the spray of bullets released a geyser of blood over Herron, the roof, the walls, and the floor. Panting from the exertion so far, but knowing he had more still to do, Herron yanked away the submachine gun as the dead operative fell. Spinning around, he unloaded what was left of the clip at another armored figure who'd appeared in the doorway, dropping him on the spot.

Five down.

Most American tactical teams – including most Tier One teams – operated in six-person units. If that was the case here, Herron knew he'd have one more enemy still roaming the house. Without question, he'd back himself one-on-one against any operator in the world, so it was time to go hunting.

He fished some spare ammo out of the vest of one of the dead men, reloaded the submachine gun with one magazine, and stuffed another in his pocket. If he'd had more time, he'd have stolen even more of their gear, but he knew every delay might come at the cost of a dead innocent. Submachine gun up in front of him, he moved through the house quickly, clearing room after room until he found the last operative.

The armored killer had his back to Herron: he seemed to have discovered Sheng and his family huddled together on the floor of a child's bedroom just seconds earlier. Without delay, Herron put several bullets into the back of the operative's knee. The man collapsed like a cheap lawn chair, screaming as he fell, his finger involuntarily squeezing on his trigger and spraying the ceiling with gunfire.

"Get them out of here, Sheng," Herron barked, aiming his weapon at the wounded man as the stunned family fled. When he was alone with the fallen agent, he spoke again. "Doing the dirty work for the Chinese, huh? I don't know which agency sent you, but they're happy to murder women and children now?"

The operative snorted and leveled a venomous glare

at Herron. "You can't hide forever, and we won't be the last team that's going to kick your door in."

Herron frowned. He'd assumed the hit squad was looking for Sheng, the man who'd foiled the Chinese invasion. Instead, it seemed Herron himself was the target. The question was why. He had assumed his service to American intelligence in stopping the Chinese invasion of Taiwan would be noted by someone, yet here an American kill team had rocked up to take him out.

It changed the calculations for him. An hour ago, he'd thought he was safe and free. Now he was on the run again.

2

───────

Back at the wheel of his car, Herron was careful to keep to the speed limit and stay mostly on back roads. The last thing he needed was a cop pulling him over, given he was now back on the radar of every intelligence service in the country.

It was just one of the million calculations he had to make now that he was a fugitive once more, a life Herron was used to, but not one he'd expected to return to so quickly.

For months, he'd been the plaything of various governments – China, the United Kingdom, the United States – who'd tried to control him, forcing him to do their bidding lest he face some terrible consequence: the death of innocents he didn't know; the false imprisonment of the one woman in the world he cared about; or a lifetime of torture and misery for him personally. Any respite he'd hoped to get by helping American intelligence had proven fleeting, but he'd learned years ago that, in this business, dwelling on the past got you killed.

After finishing the wounded operator, Herron had helped Sheng and his family get safely away, then hit the road. Settled behind the wheel of the little sedan that would carry him out of one chapter of his life and into the next, he'd headed south.

But now, after hours in transit, he needed to rest.

He pulled the car into the parking lot of an out-of-the-way motel, driving slowly past the office and the long row of rooms that comprised the straight, single-level brick establishment. It looked safe enough – there was only one guy on duty in the office, and he was staring disinterestedly at a small television on the corner of the reception desk.

He backed his car into one of the empty spaces and left the engine running, one of only three cars in the lot. He waited with one hand on the wheel, the other on the pistol in his lap, and his foot ready to hit the gas at a moment's notice. He didn't expect any threat to find him here, but if it did, he'd prefer to be at the wheel of his car rather than in a motel room.

After a full ten minutes, he hadn't even seen another car go past. Finally, he killed the engine and climbed out of the car, stuffing his pistol into the waistband of his pants and covering it with his t-shirt. It wasn't much of a hiding spot for the weapon, but given the guy in the office had been glued to his television the whole time Herron had been waiting, he doubted the receptionist had much perception of security.

He walked from the car to the office, the door chiming gently as he entered. To his surprise, the guy still didn't look up from his TV, which showed exactly how much of a damn he gave about the job. Herron paused a second or two, then cleared his throat. With a roll of his eyes, the motel staffer finally peeled his attention away from the box and looked up.

"I'd like a room." Herron plastered on his best smile, even if the other guy was acting like an asshole. "Any will do."

"They're all the same," said the staffer, whose name badge identified him as Dave. He slid a clipboard across the counter. "Fill out your details, put a hundred or a credit card on the counter, and you're good."

"There's the thing..." Herron jingled his car keys, then tossed them on the counter. "How much do you make here an hour, Dave?"

"Why the fuck do you care?" Dave shot back, but then his eyes settled on the car keys, and he slowly caught wind of what Herron was getting at. "10 bucks an hour."

"The car out there isn't much, but it's got to be worth a few weeks of shifts to you. In return, I need a room for one night."

Dave considered for a second, then reached out to push the keys back towards Herron. "Nice try, but the cleaning staff report occupancy to my boss. He'll know if someone has stayed and the money isn't paid."

"How often do they come?" Herron raised an eyebrow, taking a shot that a place this quiet might only need to employ part-time housekeeping staff, with rooms serviced every few days. "I need a break, man..."

"They come every two days, and they're due tomorrow," Dave answered. "There are four rooms needing cleaning and one guest leaving tomorrow, so my boss is going to know the exac—"

"So put me in one of the dirty rooms and tell me what time I need to leave before the cleaners arrive,"

Herron said. "I get a bed for the night, you get a car, the room gets cleaned, and your boss never finds out."

"Deal," Dave said. "But if you're not out by 7:00 am, I'm keeping the car *and* calling the cops to toss you out of here because I don't need any bullshit."

Herron nodded, and Dave removed the clipboard and the car keys from sight before putting a key on the counter. Herron scooped it up and left the office, keen to put his head on a pillow for the first time in a while. He had plans to make and threats to face tomorrow, and he wanted to do that rested. A glance back showed Dave again immersed in the television, so Herron doubted he'd change his mind about the deal.

Herron headed for his room, unlocked the door, and stepped inside. Even before he hit the light, he was regretting the bargain he'd struck. The stink hit him full in the face, a mix of weed, stale beer, farts, body odor, sex, and who the fuck knew what else. Even for a man who'd been in a lot of nasty situations, it was almost too much.

Dreading having to do so, he flicked the light switch... and discovered that the smell was the best part about the room.

The space was cramped, with peeling wallpaper and stained carpet. The yellowing curtains were drawn tight, but the light from the flickering fluorescent bulb in the ceiling was enough to reveal grime on every surface. And while Herron had slept in a lot of unpleasant places during his life, the soiled bed might be one of the worst. The bedspread was a dingy brown, and the sheets underneath looked like they hadn't been changed in weeks. The mattress was sunken in the middle, and springs poked through the thin fabric.

As for the rest of the room, a dresser with missing drawers sat against one wall with a small television perched on top, its screen covered in a layer of dust. The bathroom was no better, with a cracked sink, a dirty toilet, and a shower with a curtain that had mold growing in the folds. The detritus he'd smelled before turning on the light completed the picture, scattered on the floor and every other available surface. It was like a dumpster had been hit by a tornado.

It made him wonder if cleaners came here every other *week*, let alone every other *day*.

And that Dave the receptionist had done vastly better out of the deal.

Herron knew he should scope out the place for escape routes and weaknesses, but his exhaustion overrode both his security concerns and his dismay at the state of the place, and he collapsed onto the bed. As the springs dug into his back, he told himself he'd snooze for five minutes, then take care of the recon. His eyes grew heavy, and he plunged into a restless sleep, his dreams plagued by the faces and voices of the dead.

And after the last few weeks, there were more faces to contend with.

* * *

A LOUD NOISE outside the room jolted him awake. He sat up, immediately alert and reaching for his pistol on the bed next to him. Heart pounding, he listened intently, trying to distinguish the source of the sound. Was it just the wind, or was someone outside? If someone was there, was it just some other guest at this shithole end-of-the-road motel, or a threat?

He waited in silence, pistol aimed at the door.

During the five seconds he lay there, waiting for another showdown with a team of pissed-off, geared-up operatives, he heard no other noises. That, at least, meant the day wasn't off to the worst start, although as the light from outside peeked through a crack in the curtains, Herron desperately wished he could have another hour of sleep.

When he was satisfied that there was no team of door kickers outside, he climbed out of bed with a groan. He walked to the window and pulled back the curtain just a little, confirming with his own eyes that there was nothing to worry about; it was still dark, the same number of cars was in the lot, and there were no civilians around.

But he hadn't survived in his career this long by half-assing it.

Annoyed at himself that he hadn't done so before he'd gone to sleep, he dragged the bedside table and placed it in front of the door. Next, he stacked a bunch of the detritus from the previous occupant atop the table's surface. Cans, bottles, anything and everything that would make a racket if someone pushed the door open and knocked over his stack of crap.

It wasn't a perfect tripwire, but it'd give him a few seconds' warning if someone breached the room.

Lastly, he did a quick check of the room's windows – confirming they were all locked – and discovered that a trapdoor inside the closet was the only other entry or exit from the room. Satisfied there was only one route through which he could be attacked, he decided it was time for a shower.

He headed for the bathroom and entered the

shower stall, pistol in hand, glad for the luxury despite the perilous state of the cubicle. After running the water and finding it to be either boiling hot or freezing cold, Herron settled on the former and closed his eyes, enjoying the hot water coursing down his body even as he tried to ignore the previous occupant's soap scum and pubic hair.

He was a few minutes into the shower, and in no hurry to end it, when he heard the crack of the door being kicked in, followed by the sound of the table he'd put in the way and everything atop it crashing to the ground.

Company.

Herron stayed under the streaming water, pistol aimed at the bathroom door. Counting down four seconds, he squeezed on the trigger, unloading on whoever should be standing beyond the drawn curtain if they'd made a beeline for the sound of the running shower. He kept firing, shifting his aim slightly with each trigger pull to give himself the maximum chance of hitting whoever was on the other side.

By his third shot, the return fire started, submachine gun fire punching welts into the tiles, but then Herron's fourth round put an immediate stop to the gunfire, the thud of a body dropping to the tiled floor following a second later.

After quickly confirming he hadn't been hit, Herron slid open the shower curtain. A man lay dead, the bullet he'd taken to the face having killed him instantly. Like the crew at Sheng's house, this guy had body armor and was armed with a submachine gun, so he doubted he was working alone.

Still soaking wet, Herron moved out of the shower

and the bathroom, his pistol raised and ready for any more targets. Immediately, he was forced to retreat as bullets bit into the doorframe beside him – a second operative in the room trying to succeed where his comrade had failed.

Herron caught a quick glance at the room, confirming only two killers had come inside, meaning the rest of the hit squad – however many others – were waiting outside. They probably had cover and overlapping fields of fire, an impossible situation for him to deal with no matter how highly skilled he might be.

But he had to deal with the hostile outside the bathroom before he could worry about that.

Charging in against an opponent ready to shoot him was a suicide run, so he did the next best thing. After reaching down to pick up the dead operative's submachine gun, he lay prone on the tiled floor and emptied it into the drywall that faced the main room, keeping his own pistol in reserve. His side of the wall pocked as the operative's submachine gun tore great welts out of it. But the return fire was at chest height and went high over him...

... then ceased.

It was impossible to know whether the shooter had been hit or simply stopped to reload, but Herron had to take his chances. Rushing up off the floor, he raced for the bathroom door, pistol in hand. Diving through, gun up, he fired twice more.

The operative had just been reloading... until both Herron's shots found their mark, dropping him in a heartbeat.

Herron paused and looked around, keeping his gun

trained on the door in case the rest of the kill team tried to bull rush him. There was nothing in the room that could be used to his advantage, short of throwing diseased bed linen at them. Escape was the next best bet, so he headed for the closet and looked up at the ceiling hatch.

Grinning as a means of escape crystallized in his mind, Herron dressed quickly then pulled the shelves out of the closet to make room for his ascent. After stealing one of the operatives' submachine guns and some spare mags, he reloaded it and then pushed it up through the gap in the ceiling. Lastly, he slid his own pistol into his waistband and jumped up to grip the edge of the hatch.

He pulled himself up into the roof cavity of the motel, a cramped but long and empty crawl space filled with dust and rat droppings. It looked like there were inspection covers over every room along the motel's length. By now, the remaining operatives should have figured out he wasn't coming out, and they'd be preparing to storm his room, so he moved quickly, stopping three hatches along from where he'd entered the roof cavity. He lifted away the cover and reached down to remove some of the shelves, stacking them sideways against the closet wall. Unable to reach the lower shelves, when he climbed down, it was still a tight squeeze, but he was able to find his way into the room within a few seconds. It was in no better shape than his, but he wasn't there to conduct an inspection. Instead, he headed straight for the door.

Pistol in one hand, submachine gun in the other, he opened it.

He instantly took in the scene – two shooters

huddled behind cars, looking down their scopes at the door to his motel room, where two more shooters were standing, one on either side, about to make entry.

He took his first shot at the closest operative – one of the pair in cover – knowing that once the bullets started to fly, rooting enemies out of cover would be tricky. He fired the pistol – once, twice, three times – his shots ripping into the man's flesh.

The gunfire and the pained screams of the wounded operative alerted his comrades, and they spun and aimed at Herron, but he kept advancing, headed for the nearest of the parked vehicles. Firing his pistol at the second covered shooter to keep his head down, Herron opened up one-handed with the submachine gun at the pair who'd been at his door. Out in the open, they were forced to scramble inside the motel room, even then one of them was cut down in the hasty retreat.

It wasn't until Herron himself made it to cover that his brain registered he'd taken a hit: a bullet to the hand.

Wincing in pain, he dropped the empty pistol. With his injured hand freed up, he forced himself to ignore the burning agony as he pulled out a spare magazine for the submachine gun and slammed it into the weapon. As he did, shots from the two remaining enemy operatives left pounded into the car, smashing windows and denting panels.

Wounded, low on ammo, outnumbered, and out-positioned, Herron was desperate. A few times, he tried to pop up from behind cover and shoot back at the pair who had him pinned down, but they responded with such withering gunfire that he had no choice but to duck back again. He briefly thought about trying to open the car, climb inside, hot-wire the vehicle, and make his escape – but he figured they were good enough to see that coming.

He was trapped.

The stalemate lasted another minute, neither side able to land the killing blow or improve their situation. It was only when he heard sirens off in the distance – a lot of sirens – that Herron got the germ of an idea. He continued playing defense, firing back any time the opposing shooters got too aggressive, allowing himself a certain grim satisfaction when he tagged one of them in the arm.

Three cop cars pulled up across the street from the motel, their brakes screeching. Officers poured out, taking cover behind their cars and shouting at both Herron and the other shooters to lay down their weapons. Herron complied, lacking the benefit of any other sort of plan, putting his weapon on the ground and slowly lying down on his stomach, hands behind his back.

The operatives were less inclined to obey, which told Herron everything he needed to know about them.

They were Americans – that he was sure of – and they were off-book.

Whatever outfit they were with and whoever they worked for, their hunt for Herron hadn't been cleared with the local police department, which would likely mean all sorts of shit for them if they were captured. Herron was relying on some good old-fashioned jurisdictional confusion, the cops continuing to shout at the unidentified operatives to comply or they'd open fire.

Not only did the operatives not comply, they cut loose on the cops.

Staying low, Herron turned his head to the side so he could see the exchange of fire. The operatives hammered the cops with the same volume of submachine gun fire that had kept Herron pinned. The difference was the number of cops – too many cops, too well covered – to repeat the same tactic indefinitely. So when the law enforcement officers returned fire, they cut down one shooter, then the other.

Silence descended over the makeshift battlefield for just a moment, then the cops surged toward the parking lot. A pair of them dealt with Herron, one putting a knee on his back and a gun to his head while the other cuffed him, taking little care with his wounded hand. Herron didn't resist, because the safest place for him in the world right now was probably inside a jail cell.

Herron waited while they read him his Miranda rights, then cooperated as they lifted him up off the ground and frog-marched him to one of the pockmarked squad cars. As they escorted him away, he spotted a security camera concealed among some overgrown trees. It was peering down on the parking lot, right where he'd parked his car, something he should have seen the night before but was easily missed in the darkness. It explained how the operatives had tracked him to the motel. Clearly, whoever the goons worked for had access to the footage, and they'd made him.

It showed Herron the industrial-sized pile of shit he was in, although his own tired carelessness had compounded it.

The cops seemed to show little care for the bullet wound to his hand until one of them appeared from the motel reception with a few kitchen towels and offered some rudimentary first aid, a few towels acting as the pad, the others as the bandage.

"Fantastic," Herron sighed, seated in the back of the squad car, cuffed and with his wounded hand throbbing like crazy.

"We're going to take you to the hospital to get that looked at," said one of the two cops who climbed into the front of the car. "Don't give us any shit."

"Deal," Herron said, sitting back in the seat, content to have a moment of safety.

The rest – evading the operatives after him and getting to Kearns – could wait.

3

It had been almost a decade since Herron had been in a hospital bed. As a member of the Enclave, then a man on the run, he'd been denied even the simplest measures of self-care, among them the ability to see a medical professional to treat a wound. Instead, he'd been forced to rely on shady backroom butchers to patch him up. Now he'd been picked up by the cops, however, he could again enjoy the luxury of proper treatment even before they asked him a single question about the shootout.

"God bless America," he whispered to himself.

He was seated in an emergency room suite, one of a dozen that ringed a central nurses' station. Each housed patients sporting various ailments, accompanied by some family members or friends to keep the occupant company. One had Herron, handcuffed to the rail of his bed, and a pair of cops standing at his door.

At least he hadn't waited long to be seen. There seemed to be an unwritten rule that when the cops brought in a perp, a swarm of doctors and nurses would descend to get the troublesome bastard out of the hospital and away to the police station as quickly as possible. As soon as Herron had sat on the bed, he'd had a doctor see to him. A few minutes after that, the nurse who'd accompanied the doc had started his treatment.

"Hope *they* didn't do this to you," she said, gesturing with her chin at the door, where the cops hovered watchfully. "Or, if they did, that you deserved it."

"It was another guy, but you should see what they did to him," Herron said, then watched her work for a moment before asking, "Is there going to be any permanent damage? Or any need for surgery?"

"The bullet went clean through, which helps," she replied, "but that's probably a question for one of the doctors. We're backed up right now though. For now, they just want me to clean and dress the wound."

Herron knew the cops wouldn't wait for him to have that surgical consult – after his first meeting with the doc, he'd overheard them tell the nurse to do enough to stop him from bleeding out, after which he'd be hauled in for questioning. It was probably against his civil rights, but he wasn't exactly in a great position to argue, given he was one of the most wanted men in America.

If the cops had known his name, or if one of them had seen his face on one of the million Most Wanted bulletins he'd featured in, he'd be put into FBI custody, and the feds would throw him into the deepest, darkest cell they had. They'd only open it again when it was time to hose out his remains and get the cell ready for the next poor sucker.

"Well, I'm not in any hurry," he said.

"Sure," the nurse said with a smile. "Anyway,

regarding recovery, I'm not sure. Some heal fine, but others..."

"Others stay screwy?"

"How much it affects people depends on the type of life they lead. What do you do?"

"I'm a... uh... in waste management."

"Like a garbage collector?" She locked eyes on him, waiting for a response.

"I'm engaged in the entire spectrum, from identification to sorting to disposal. It's very fulfilling."

The nurse finished up in silence, put the instruments she'd been using back on the trolley, and removed her surgical gloves. "Cleaned, disinfected, stitched, dressed, bandaged. You want some painkillers?"

"I'd like some, but I'll pass," Herron said, with some regret. "I had a problem with those things a few years ago, so I try to avoid them now."

"Sir, you've been shot..." Her voice trailed off, as if she couldn't believe what she was hearing. "Are you sure? Because once I walk out of here—"

"The cops are going to march me away to the station," he finished. Slowly, he moved his wounded hand under his T-shirt and lifted it to reveal a host of burns and scars. "I'm a frequent flyer."

"You've got your own damn plane," the nurse said, wide-eyed. "You're lucky you're still alive at all, after all that punishment."

"Taking out the trash really takes it out of you. I appreciate your help to patch me up."

"You're welcome," she said, then got up, washed her hands, and left the room without another word.

Alone again in the suite, Herron closed his eyes and

rested; he guessed he had a few seconds until the cops manhandled him back to the squad car. He gave no thought to escaping, because he had no way out of the cuffs – his time would be best spent conserving energy until he caught a break. Besides, his hand was throbbing, and he was relishing this moment of quiet after two grueling gunfights in twelve hours.

The cops took longer than he'd expected. When at last the suite door opened, they approached him without saying a thing. One of the cops kept a watchful eye on him while the other cop unlocked the cuffs securing him to the hospital bed and then cuffed Herron's hands in front of him. After that, they dragged him to his feet, each gripped an arm, and they marched him through the emergency room toward the exit.

Herron felt eyes on him, curious members of the public rubbernecking as they walked. For a man used to staying in the shadows, it was like he suddenly had a spotlight pointed at him, like everyone knew who he was and everyone wanted him dead. He couldn't do anything to shake that feeling or to change the situation right now, but he wanted to do it soon.

They headed down the corridor, both cops keeping one hand on one of his arms, and the other hand on their holstered pistols. Whether they were expecting an ambush or an escape attempt, Herron wasn't sure, but it was clear they were anxious. Their eyes darted around, checking every room they passed and sizing up every person they saw. They may not know who Herron was, but they knew he was someone.

Taking down a team of heavily armed operatives was a decent hint at that.

They were almost to the main lobby when one of

the hands on his arms clenched tight, the officer pulling back on him. Herron staggered, barely finding his feet in time to avoid tripping. The cop who had been holding him toppled forward, giving Herron a view of the back of his head.

And the hole in it.

As the cop dropped, Herron jerked his arm free in one violent motion, right as the second officer was figuring out his partner had been shot. Herron helped him along by shouting: "Move!"

But his escort didn't have Herron's training, or his reflexes. He barely got his gun out of its holster before he too fell dead. Two cops had been downed by two perfect headshots in less than two seconds, leaving Herron cuffed and alone.

Even as he moved, Herron's brain was working the angles. The wounds were small caliber because the hallway hadn't been sprayed from exit wounds, and he hadn't heard the shots, or even had any sense he was a target. Whoever had him in his sights was a professional – having chosen the right location and the right tools for an ambush that caught Herron totally off guard.

He reached down to tear the pistol from the holster of the first cop who'd fallen, before retrieving the keys to the cuffs – he'd taken careful note of where the cop had stashed them after unlocking him from the hospital bed, his hands moving quickly to the correct belt pouch. All the while, his eyes desperately searched for the shooter, and a second later, he spotted the killer's nest.

Overhead, one ceiling tile had been slid back a few inches, a sight so innocuous in the aging hospital that even Herron would never have noticed it. From there, the shooter could have taken out the cops, then slipped away in the roof before Herron could locate and respond to the threat. And given the skill of the ambush and the precision of the shooting, it raised a question.

If the shooter had wanted Herron dead, his would have been the first head to take a bullet.

So why was he still alive?

Did he have an ally he didn't know about?

That would sure make a change...

As he unlocked the cuffs, Herron thought about going after the shooter, but a squeal from the end of the hallway sealed the deal for him. A woman who'd spotted the carnage was now running back the way she had come, towards the reception area.

And hospital security.

Herron turned and ran the other way, deeper into the hospital. He had a few options now, but none were very promising. The woman's story would bring cops and security down on him like flies on shit, given it would look obvious to any casual observer that *he'd* killed the cops.

In response, he was armed, so shooting his way out was an option, but he didn't want to gun down law enforcement in a hospital lobby full of children and sick people. So he decided to do the best thing he could in the circumstances.

Checking each door he passed, he finally ducked into a storage space for surgical supplies. Looking over his shoulder the whole time, he donned scrubs, a gown, mask, and cap, and surgical gloves. Pocketing the pistol, he loaded up a surgical trolley with some random gear and then pushed it out into the hallway.

To any passers-by, he'd look like a nurse or an orderly on the way to a surgical suite.

He pushed the trolley through the hospital, desperate to find an exit. He took a left and then a right, the maze of corridors seemingly endless. A few staff members took notice of him as he moved through their ranks, but none were suspicious enough to challenge him or raise the alarm with hospital security.

At last, he saw a sign for an exit. Although he'd lost his bearings a little, he thought he was at the east end of the building, which should mean the way out would take him close to the parking lot. But seconds before he reached the door, an alarm wailed, overlaid with an announcement over the public address system.

The hospital was being locked down because of a security incident.

"Fuck that," Herron said.

Herron dumped the trolley near the door, added a scalpel to the arsenal in his pockets, and then kept moving. Opening the door, he peered outside: the coast was clear, a well-manicured lawn separating him from the parking lot, where stealing a car would be his ticket to freedom. He would figure out the rest later.

He set off, relying on his disguise to keep him concealed for a little longer, but halfway across the lawn, he sensed he was being followed. He kept going – to turn would invite attention if it were law enforcement following him – trusting his senses to alert him if the person on his tail got any closer.

Reaching the high-rise parking garage, he stopped at the elevator and pressed the button to ascend. But when he realized the elevator car would take too long to arrive – and with his tail getting ever closer – Herron switched, taking the stairs. He climbed one flight, then another, then another, using switchbacks of the flights of steps to flush out his tail. If someone really was on his ass, they'd follow him up the stairs, due to the risk of losing him if they took the elevator and chose the wrong floor.

Arriving at the top, he gripped the handle of the stairwell door, peering through the slit of dirty glass to the parking garage beyond. He couldn't see anyone waiting for him, nor had anyone come up the stairs behind him, but that guaranteed nothing. Sliding his undamaged hand into his pocket, he took hold of the pistol, ready to draw it if necessary. Then, with his recently dressed hand, he pushed open the door.

There, in front of the elevator, someone was waiting for him.

"You," Herron snarled.

"Me," the man said. "Been a long time, Mitch."

"I thought you were dead."

"I should be. But you were never going to get rid of me that easily."

The first time Herron had encountered the man known as Shade, he'd barely escaped with his life – the Enclave super-assassin had proven himself far more skilled than Herron, who had been caught flat-footed by his opponent.

But Herron had escaped, taking his chance to dismantle the Enclave, destroy the Master and – he thought – put an end to Shade himself. Facing off with his nemesis on top of a building, Herron's last battle with the ice-cold killer had ended when Shade had fallen from the roof.

There was no way he had ever expected their paths would cross again.

"You're a cockroach," Herron spat.

"You're kind of hard to kill yourself, Mitch. We aren't all that different."

"No, you reveled in the carnage you got to inflict as part of the Enclave."

"And then you spoiled the fun."

"What is it you want, Shade?"

"You can imagine how upset I was, after waking up from the nine-month coma you left me in, to find you left everything a shambles, Mitch. Everything I enjoyed most about my life – gone," Shade snarled. "But hey, I thought you were dead, so I went about rebuilding things. Got a fair way along that road before you appeared on the radar in Hong Kong."

"So why not shoot me in the hallway with those cops?"

Shade laughed. "Because I've dreamt of this moment for years. If I wanted to put a bullet in you, I'd have done it. But no, for you, for me – for us – it needs to be messy and visceral. When they come to clean up the mess after our last fight, I want them to be disgusted by the blood, the gore, the violence. I want to prove once and for all who's the best man. That what happened on that rooftop was a mistake of destiny."

"Then let's do it," Herron said, tired of the chatter.

"I love it when you talk dirty," Shade smirked, drawing a simple flick-knife from his pocket. "Got a blade?"

Herron reached into his coat for the scalpel. "Knives it is."

And then it was on.

Shade lunged, aiming a thrust for the heart, but Herron moved fast, sidestepping the attack and responding with a swipe of his scalpel. He missed – barely – and Shade hopped back a step.

"Either of those moves would have gutted just about anyone else on Earth," Shade said, grinning. "Nice to see you haven't lost your touch."

He advanced again, always the aggressor, stabbing forward rapidly, forcing Herron back on the defensive. Some strikes he dodged, others he parried, the metal of their blades ringing as they met. Slowly retreating under the onslaught of Shade's overwhelming skill and aggression, Herron found his back against the wall – literally – the concrete of the parking garage rough and cold.

"Nowhere to run," Shade said, letting up his attack just long enough to delight in his impending victory.

Herron didn't respond. As Shade came for him, he parried the thrust, pushing the blade aside, then gripping Shade's wrist with his own free hand. Then, using the assassin's momentum against him, he tripped Shade and sent him stumbling to the ground.

The advantage was fleeting, Shade rolling and coming up on his feet.

He charged at Herron, his blade finally finding flesh, delivering a nick to Herron's side. But there was no time to worry about the wound – dwelling on it would allow Shade to bury the knife deeper into him. Instead, Herron used his forearm to swat Shade's hand aside, then kicked out, his boot planting firmly in his foe's chest. Shade staggered backward, buying Herron some breathing space.

Back and forth, thrust and parry. Herron was an elite operative, feared the world over for his capabilities, matched by few, but Shade was something else. As an

Alpha – one of the top-tier operatives of the Enclave – he'd been more than a match for any single human on Earth, and had proven before he was more than a match for Herron. In a fair fight, Shade would take him down eventually.

The fight ranged through the parking lot, in amongst parked sedans and SUVs, with windows smashed and bodywork dented as the combatants slammed each other back and forth. Both men were fit, but both were soon sweating profusely and puffing. Herron got cut several times in the exchanges, Shade too, but none of the injuries were bad enough to slow or kill either. Their offensive skill was matched by their defensive prowess, each man a fortress that was hard to penetrate.

Until Herron tripped.

Falling backward and landing on his ass, Herron instinctively put his injured hand out to brace his fall, his landing sent spears of agony out through his wound. Even in pain, his other hand brandished the scalpel out to ward off any assault by Shade, but Herron knew the mistake was fatal.

No operative, no matter how well-trained, could totally free themselves from reacting to extreme pain. Most could suppress it a little, some could resist its use as a torture tactic, and a few could fight on despite it, but none could ignore it completely.

And that was all a man as skilled and as ruthless as Shade needed.

A split-second.

Immediately registering Herron's vulnerability, the Enclave's former top operative moved in for the kill. Eschewing the knife, he took a step forward and planted his boot atop Herron's wounded hand, grinding down on it.

The explosion of pain was indescribable, stunning Herron, taking his breath away in a ragged gasp.

"The natural order restored," Shade said, as he ripped the scalpel from Herron's grasp and put his own blade to the defeated man's neck. "That was a better workout than I expected, though."

Herron could do nothing to resist. There was no great escape on offer, no cunning trick to turn the tables; an operative as skilled as Shade was well-versed in anything he might try. He could do nothing as Shade drew the knife across his throat – gently, almost tenderly, a deadly caress.

Then he stopped, the expected pressure to open Herron's arteries failing to come.

Shade stood and took a step back. "Go, Mitch. But know that I beat you, and I can do it again."

Herron looked up at him in disbelief. "Why?"

"Because I've proved my point," Shade replied. "And there's more profit in keeping you alive for now."

4

———

Herron tapped the wheel of the car in time with the beat of the music, hating the song but glad for its help in keeping him awake. Even with it, he could feel fatigue overtaking him and kept his eyes wide and blinking as wind battered his face, rushing in from the four open windows. He had been driving for eight hours from the hospital in Washington D.C. without knowing exactly where he was going, but he would have to stop for a rest soon.

Still, he had achieved his goal of putting significant distance between himself and the operatives on his tail, not to mention Shade. The assassin's return had changed everything – the most sadistic motherfucker Herron had ever had the misfortune to encounter was back on the hunt, and he would have to deal with that, even if it killed him. But first, he needed time to rest, recuperate, and plan. For that, he was heading out of the city for somewhere remote.

It was most likely the hit teams – and Shade – had tracked him using the large numbers of security cameras in the nation's capital, so moving himself to rural America should mean fewer electronic eyeballs searching for him. It might not be perfect, but it ought to give him the breathing room he needed, and it was the best plan he could come up with right now.

The darkness of the rural interstate wasn't helping with his tiredness, interrupted only sporadically by the bright lights of a car coming the other way, but after a few more miles he saw a sign highlighting a truck stop up ahead. Taking the exit, he soon found himself in the parking lot of a gas station with a diner. There was nowhere to sleep, but at least he could eat and freshen up.

He filled the tank then parked the vehicle, and as he climbed out he did a physical stock take. His throbbing hand burned like fire, distracting him from the dull aches in the rest of his battered body. It was a sad state to be in if Shade or more teams of operatives found him, but he was hoping he had slipped the net for now.

Standing in the parking lot, he quickly scanned for security cameras, relieved when his practiced eyes could not locate any. Inside the diner, it was the same story – whoever owned this slice of rural heaven was more trusting than they should be. He sat in one booth, the stiff leather cracked and faded in spots, and waited until the server came over to him.

"Never seen you 'round here," she said, putting a cup of coffee and a menu in front of him, her voice curious rather than accusatory. "Passing through?"

"Yeah," Herron said, engaging just enough to be polite. Then, without picking up the menu, he unloaded an order that shouldn't be a problem at any greasy spoon across America. "Toast, scrambled eggs, bacon."

The server nodded and shuffled off, reading Herron's signal that he wasn't in the mood to chat. She'd get all sorts passing through: from truckers who wanted to talk because it would be their only conversation that day to drivers who wanted to eat in peace. She had done what she had to do, then retreated, and it struck Herron that, in some ways, it wasn't too dissimilar to his methods – get the job done and get out.

Or in this case, he had fought and killed, and now he was on the run.

The food came a few minutes later, and as he worked his way through it he continued the deep brooding that had kept his mind busy in the car. Disbelief at Shade's return, disgust that he had yet again failed to best the man who had cost him so much, and doubt about what his next move should be. For a man used to being the aggressor, he hated being on the back foot.

Shade was probably the last of the Enclave's Alphas left alive. The others were either killed alongside the Master in the final shootout that had eradicated the organization or would have perished in the years since. It was Herron's duty – his legacy – to finish the job he had started so many years ago. Hiding out in rural America was necessary for now, but it only delayed him from reaching that goal.

More than that, he wanted to find out why the former Enclave assassin had let him live.

Profit.

Shade was the ultimate killer, skilled and ruthless, but Herron had never known him to care about *profit*.

His hand pulsed with pain again. It had already been in bad shape after being shot, but Shade stomping on it would have caused all sorts of additional damage. He needed to get it looked at, but there was only one place he thought he might be safe right now and only one person he trusted to keep watch if he closed his eyes to sleep.

While Herron didn't know exactly where she was, he knew was how to find her.

When he was done eating, he pushed his plate away and drained his coffee. Then he waited. The place wasn't very busy, with only a few tired-looking truckers taking a break between long stretches of driving, but there was just the one server, and it took some time before she came around his way again. When she came to take his plate, she flashed him a smile.

He didn't return it.

"I've got a gun in my bag," Herron whispered, fixing her with a hard gaze even as her eyes widened. "But you'll never even see it, as long as you keep quiet and listen carefully to my instructions, okay?"

She nodded, fear in her eyes.

"Okay—" Herron read the name on the badge she was wearing. "—Carol. I want you to know I'm not going to hurt you or rob the diner, but there's something I need. Now I'm betting the jerk behind the counter who pinched your ass on the way over here has a gun tucked away back there. Right?"

She nodded again.

"So, that bozo is going to look over here in a moment and wonder why you're spending so much time with me. He's also going to wonder why you look scared, so I need you to pretend to laugh while I'm telling you what I need."

She laughed, obviously fake but passably enough

that when the man behind the counter looked over, he simply frowned and looked away again.

"Well done," Herron said. "Now, I need a laptop or a phone that's connected to the internet. Any one will do. Do you have a personal cell phone or something like that around here that you could access without alerting your boss?"

She nodded. And laughed.

"Go get it. And please don't think about running, screaming, or going for the gun yourself." Herron paused to let the words sink in. "I've got military training, and you'll both be dead – unnecessarily – before you know it. Okay?"

She nodded again.

"Good. When I've got the computer or a phone, I'll only need it for a few minutes. While I use it, you can go about your work as usual, but I want to see you at all times. If I lose sight of you, I'm going to assume the worst and start shooting."

She gulped, her face pale.

"When I'm done with the computer or the phone, I'll leave it right here, along with a very large tip. Then I'll get up, walk out, and drive away. You'll never know I was here unless you do something stupid. Now get to it."

Herron watched Carol as she shuffled away, totally ignoring a customer who was trying to get her attention as she passed. She stood at the counter for a moment, glancing nervously at Herron and then at her boss before reaching under the counter. Her hands were out of sight for a few seconds, then she stuffed something into her pocket.

As she started back towards Herron, he kept a close

eye on her, his uninjured hand resting on the grip of his pistol. He didn't want a shootout and wouldn't do anything to hurt the server or her boss, but if she'd been stupid enough to get the gun instead of a phone, he'd have to rely on being able to draw faster than her... before bolting out of the diner.

His worry was proven misplaced when, a moment later, she pulled out a battered iPhone and put it on the table. "It's old, but it works. The code is four ones."

Herron nodded. "Stay within sight for the next few minutes. I'll do what I need to do, then you're in the clear and can forget I was ever here."

He waited while she moved away from the table and went back to work, leaving the phone untouched as he watched her, the guy behind the counter, and the other patrons. The diner was as sleepy and calm as it had been before he'd made his move, just quiet chatter and background music. If there was a threat here, it had bested Herron's considerable detection skills.

Finally, he picked up the phone, unlocked it, and went to work. Opening a web browser, he found his way to a popular email site, then punched in a username and password. As his finger hovered over the 'login' button, he hoped Kearns had set up the account like he'd told her to, the last time he'd stolen a phone. The username was the first man he'd killed in her presence; the password, the place they'd last separated.

Username: Tiny12345@gmail.com

Password: McDonalds.

The old phone seemed to take an eternity to process the login, but eventually, it accepted the credentials and proceeded to the email inbox. Relieved, Herron saw there was one message, untitled and unread. It had been sent by the same account – a message meant for nobody except Herron if he survived, destined to be unread forever if he hadn't.

He clicked on it.

Again, the phone took its time. When the email opened, it contained nothing but an address, and Herron used the browser to look up the address. He'd told Erica to flee somewhere remote and off-grid, and he was pleased to see his own ideas about that kind of place closely matched hers. From what he could tell, she was holed up in a small shack off a dirt road in the most rural part of rural West Virginia.

It was perfect.

Herron read the address and considered the map one more time, committing it to memory, then he cleared the browser and the map of its cache. Now he had somewhere to go, he wanted to get back on the road. He placed the phone and some cash on the table then, without making eye contact with the server, stood up and walked out.

A quick look around confirmed no hit teams had caught up with him while he'd been eating, so Herron indulged himself in a few moments of fresh air, strolling leisurely across the parking lot. When he reached his car, he unlocked it, climbed inside, gunned the engine, and pulled away, feeling a hell of a lot livelier than he had when he'd left the hospital.

For the first time in a long time, it was like he was going home.

* * *

HERRON'S HEADLIGHTS were the only thing illuminating the dark forest road as he slowly traversed it, the gravel crunching under his wheels. Navigating on his memory of the map alone, he hoped he hadn't missed a turn or taken a wrong one, because the forest shack was about as far off the radar as a place could be and still have a street address.

As he got closer, the thought of seeing Erica Kearns for the first time in years filled him with excitement and dread. Excitement because she'd come to mean a lot to him in the brief time they'd spent together. Dread because he'd committed to never seeing her again for a reason – her safety – and breaking that commitment could bring danger to her door.

But he had little choice. He needed somewhere safe to bunker down – to plan and to heal – and he knew of no better place to do it than by her side. Being close to her also meant he could keep her safe, he told himself. With Shade back in the field, the threat to Kearns' safety had amplified a hundredfold. The Alpha had targeted her once to get to Herron, and he wouldn't hesitate to do so again.

At last, Herron spotted a small sign for the street she lived on, a right turn between dense trees on either side of the road. Keeping his eyes peeled, he passed several mailboxes and driveways, spaced every few miles and no doubt leading to similar small, off-the-grid shacks to the one where Kearns had holed up. The numbers counted upwards... 24... 25... 26... On and on, until he reached the end of the winding road.

Kearns' hideout didn't exist.

Herron turned the car around and drove back, paying closer attention this time.

Then he saw it, a small turnoff, barely visible in the dark. He smiled to himself – Kearns had the last address on the road, and must have removed the mailbox for her shack. It was a simple countermeasure, meant to fool the casual observer, and, for a moment, it had fooled Herron.

He turned onto the mystery driveway and found the building a mile back from the road, protected from sight by the thick array of trees and the winding driveway. Lit up by his headlights, it looked old yet well-built, but totally abandoned. There was no car in the driveway, no lights were on; there was no sign at all that it was inhabited.

But Herron knew better.

Killing the engine but keeping the headlights on, he climbed out of the car. For a few minutes, he watched the house, waiting for someone to emerge to investigate the disturbance. He had his pistol close to hand if he needed it – if he'd made a mistake and this wasn't Kearns' place, he'd rather face any threat from a distance than knock on the door and have some hillbilly open it a crack and unload a shotgun into his face.

Nobody emerged from the house.

Finally, Herron decided he'd have to chance Billy Bob and his shotgun, or he was never going to get answers. If Erica was here, he was proud of her for staying holed up inside and not sticking her neck out to investigate who'd arrived in the dead of night. But if she wasn't, then he didn't know what the hell he'd do next.

Holding the pistol by his side, he slowly approached the house, staying in the middle of the beam of the headlights; anyone quickly opening the door might be blinded enough by them to give him a precious second to act. He stepped up onto the porch and pounded on the simple wooden door. Nobody answered. Herron waited, then tried again, this time thumping the door loud enough to wake the dead.

He stopped just in time to hear someone pump a shotgun. A figure emerged from the darkness to stand six feet away from him. Herron kept his pistol at his side – not even he was fast enough to beat a quick trigger pull and a load of buckshot at this range.

"Erica?" he asked hopefully, unable to see who was holding the gun, his trick with the bright headlights now working against him.

"Didn't think you'd end up here, Mitch," Kearns said, relief clear in her voice. "After the last time we spoke, I thought for sure you were going to end up dead."

Herron turned his head to face her, although he kept the rest of his body frozen in place. "Well, I pulled off the impossible."

"As usual," she said. Closing the distance to him, she laid the shotgun down on the porch floor, then wrapped him in a hug. "It's good to see you, Mitch."

He hugged her back. "You too. I'd been hoping to come here and tell you completing that mission had removed the danger."

"But?"

"But now there's more danger than ever."

"For me?"

"And me." He stepped out of the hug. "There are government operatives on my tail. And…"

She studied his face as he hesitated. "Go on."

"Shade is back. He's after me, which means he's after you too."

Erica blinked a few times as she absorbed the news. "Sounds like you've really stayed off the radar..."

"Let's head inside, and I'll explain everything that's happened since I saw you last."

She led them inside. Entering the shack she'd called home for the last few weeks, Herron saw it was simple and rustic. The main room was dominated by a large stone fireplace – currently without a fire – while the walls were made of rough-hewn logs. A thick rug covered the wooden floorboards, and a pair of sofas dominated the far corner, placed around a coffee table. A bookcase covered one wall, filled with well-worn paperbacks, jars of homemade preserves, and cans of food. There was a simple kitchen – with a few pots and pans hanging from hooks overhead, ready for use on the small wood-burning stove – plus a functional cabinet, and a washbasin and pitcher to complete the setup. A ladder in the corner led up to a loft, where a simple bed made up with wool blankets and pillows looked out through a small window over the forest. A small lantern hung from a nail in the ceiling, casting a warm glow throughout, the lack of visible light outside explained by internal shutters enclosing every window.

It had all the simple amenities Herron would need for a few months in the wilderness to heal and plan.

But one thing nagged at him.

"How'd you get outside to bail me up with the shotgun?" He looked around. "There's no other door, and there's no way you got outside quickly enough when I drove up to the house."

"Trapdoor," she said, pointing to the kitchen.

In the dim light, Herron could see a small hatch in the wall. The hinges were well hidden, and there was no handle – all he could make out was the cut of the doorframe. He walked closer and pressed against it; the hatch swung open. Herron frowned. He didn't want a shooter to come in the door and get the drop on them the same way Erica had surprised him outside.

"Hold on a minute," he said and dragged the cabinet from the kitchen in front of it. It wasn't perfect, but it plugged the hole in their defenses, and he could move it to get them out if he needed to.

With that done, Erica led him over to one sofa before retreating to the small kitchen area. After some time and a little noise, she carried over two cups of coffee, put one in front of him, and cradled the other as she sat down on the other sofa. She took a sip, curled her legs up under her like a cat, and locked eyes on him. The message was obvious.

She wanted answers.

"How'd you find this place?" Herron asked, trying to start the conversation with a little small talk. "Looks far cozier than anything I thought you'd find at short notice."

"An old colleague of mine at the CDC was convinced some virus or another was going to wipe out humanity, so he kept a small, well-stocked shack up here. He died last year, and he had no family. Left the place to me." She leveled her gaze on him. "Now come on, Mitch. Spill it."

Herron started at the beginning. He told her about how he'd left the United States, killed the Master, and destroyed the Enclave. He told her about his life on the run after that, keeping a low profile until trouble had found him. He told her about the threats he'd faced down and about overcoming China's attempts to control several of its Pacific neighbors and the islands of Hong Kong and Taiwan.

Finally, he told her about the reason he'd been forced to send her into hiding, the threat against her life by the U.S. Government.

"Assholes," Kearns muttered. "After you prevented a catastrophe from sweeping the country, you'd assume they'd let bygones be bygones. What happened to your hand?"

"Shot. Hurt my ego more than anything else, but I need to lie low while it heals. That, and to reduce the heat on me a little. They keep finding me, and I don't know how."

"Security cameras?"

"Maybe, but I've been evading those for years, so I'm not sure what's changed. Suddenly, no matter how careful I am, they end up on my tail. I'm hoping somewhere this remote is off their radar."

"So they might come here?"

"I was careful to protect the location as best I could, but yes. Normally, I can be sure if I've been followed or not, but the last two times they found me..."

"So I should go?"

"Probably."

She shivered a little. Herron put his coffee down and headed for the fireplace. He arranged some kindling and logs, his back to Kearns. He felt her eyes boring into him as he struck a match and held it to the kindling, watching as the flames slowly took hold. Soon the fire crackled and popped, casting shadows on the walls of the cabin and promising warmth before too long.

He returned to the sofa and smiled at her. "Better?"

"Much," she said.

They settled into silence again, and she took her time sipping her coffee before slowly uncurling her body and leaning forward. She put her cup on the coffee table, stood, and switched sofas so she could sit next to him. The silence stretched out, as if each was waiting for the other to speak, then Kearns did what few people had ever achieved when matched against Herron.

She took the initiative from him.

She moved slowly, giving him plenty of time to pull away if he wanted to, then moving in when it was clear he wanted what was coming. She kissed him gently, their eyes open and locked on each other, the flames from the fire reflecting in their eyes. When finally she pulled away, she left Herron fighting every one of his old instincts, every bit of experience and training and logic that shouted for him to stop.

He'd come here to rest and recuperate and to protect Erica. Now he was about to commit the cardinal sin for a field operative – getting involved with someone who could be used against you, who could be hurt to hurt you. The voices in the back of his brain, screaming their warnings at him, had kept him alive in a job that killed most by the age of thirty-five – he'd be insane to ignore them.

But ignore them he did. Without a word, he leaned in and pressed his lips to hers again. She responded eagerly, their tongues entwining. He wrapped his arms tightly around her, pulling her closer until she was practically sitting on his lap. She ran her fingers through his hair while he savored the feel of his lips on hers.

Tomorrow – and the consequences – be damned.

When they finally broke apart, gasping for breath, Herron spoke first. "So what now?"

"Be with me tonight," she whispered, her voice husky. "I missed you when you were gone, Mitch. I thought about you every day. I worried about you every day. Let me have one night where I don't have to."

He rose from the sofa, held her hand, and led her up to the loft.

Where the bed waited.

5

Herron's eyes shot open.

As his hand reached out to seize the pistol he'd left on the bedside table, he held his breath, listening for a repeat of the sound that had woken him. His mind was screaming there was a threat, and while he'd ignored his inner voice about sleeping with Kearns, he wasn't going to this time.

Despite Erica clearly wanting him to.

She snuggled in close, resting her head on his bare chest. "Stop being so paranoid, Mitch, there's nothing within a mile of us."

"I thought the same at a motel where I got shot," he replied, a little more tersely than he intended. "I'm going to go check it out."

"Fine," she said, squeezing him tight, then she rolled over and reached into the drawer of her own bedside table. "Take this..."

The Colt 45 she handed him was more powerful than the pistol he'd taken from the cop. He checked the load, satisfied himself that it was full, then climbed up from the bed. "Thanks. Stay here."

With the cop's pistol in his injured hand and the hand-cannon in the other, he walked to the edge of the loft, looking down on the front door. If there really was a threat outside, there was only one way into the cabin – the front door – and he had a fantastic over-watch position from which to defend it.

He wasn't worried about the windows thanks to the sturdy internal shutters

The thick log walls of the shack should take any bullets

And he'd blocked Kearns' escape hatch.

The place was a fortress.

He was tempted to take a quick look outside and then return to the warmth of the bed and Kearns' body, but before he could, the door flew open with a crash, a battering ram taking it off its hinges. Two shooters led the way in, their submachine guns sweeping the interior of the small shack for a target.

Herron gave them no time to determine the layout or discover there was a second level to the building. The first they knew of that was when he fired the Colt, once, twice. The gun recoiled like no other pistol could, but the result was worth it.

The rounds hit the attackers like a truck, tearing large wounds on the way in and even larger ones on the way out. Everything in between was devastated. The intruders hit the floor, dead before they even knew where the shots were coming from.

The first pair dealt with, Herron quickly slid down the ladder, trading caution for time. He wanted to fully seize the initiative before those left outside could reorganize. Because, with Kearns still sheltering in the loft, his only thought was eradication of the enemy.

His feelings for Erica were additional fuel for his fury.

He wouldn't call it love because he didn't know what that felt like. People in his line of work had fundamental flaws in their emotions, enabling them to do what most would find unthinkable. But something new was driving him forward, ready to unleash the most devastating violence.

He'd hidden her to keep her safe. He'd gone on the run to keep her safe. He'd agreed to all manner of subterfuge to keep her safe. And now he was prepared to kill anyone who put her at risk.

Reaching ground level, he burst outside and into the darkness. The gunfire he'd expected didn't come, giving him a slight chance, but moving from the firelight inside the log cabin robbed him of his night vision. Swiftly, he took shelter behind his car while his eyes adjusted.

As he waited, he listened for any hint of more enemies and where they might be. It wasn't difficult to pinpoint them: they were shouting in panicked voices and running through the forest, making no effort to conceal their retreat. Whoever they were, they hadn't expected the sort of reception he'd given them.

Was it possible they hadn't expected Herron at all?

Had they come for Kearns?

The thought sparked fury in the pit of his stomach. Throwing caution to the wind, he bounded through the forest like a gazelle; he wasn't quiet, not by his usual standard, but he was nowhere near as loud as the retreating thugs who'd sought to invade his sanctum and kill Erica.

Around half a mile from the house, he caught up with them. By then, his vision had adjusted, and there was just enough moonlight penetrating the tree canopy that he could see their silhouettes moving away in the darkness.

He had no qualms about killing men who were retreating. He wouldn't harm civilians if he could help it, but anyone who took unprovoked hostile action against him or Kearns was fair game, so he leveled the Colt and started firing. The shot boomed, the thug dropped, and he shifted aim and downed another.

If the retreating goons hadn't heard Herron on their tail, making enough noise themselves to wake the dead, they knew he was here now. And they responded with gunfire.

A lot.

Herron ducked behind a trunk as a submachine gun opened up in his direction, punching into the surrounding trees. What surprised him was the duration of the gunfire: shooters blazing away and burning ammo, rather than taking the tightly controlled shots he'd expect from professionals.

Combined with their lax entry discipline and their comical retreat, this told Herron all he needed to know. This wasn't a group of tier-one operatives, nor had they simply not realized Herron was in the shack. Unlike the other teams that had hit him in the last day or two, these weren't professionals at all.

Back toward the house, a shotgun boomed, loud even over the clatter of the submachine guns.

He paused for a second until enough of the shooters

ran out of ammunition and the torrent of incoming lead reduced to a trickle. Popping out from behind cover, he fired in the general direction of the gunfire: four shots—two from the cop's pistol and two from the big Colt 45.

Immediately, he turned and ran toward the shack.

He moved with even less care for his own safety than before, sprinting through the forest, unsure if what remained of the hit team was giving chase. If they followed him, he would deal with them later. What worried him more was something back at the house had caused Kearns to fire her shotgun – an unknown threat that had only moved in once Herron had gone after the retreating stooges.

Back at the cabin, nothing seemed immediately amiss – there were no shooters, no vehicles had arrived while he'd been gone, and there were no voices or gunfire to help him locate a target. The place looked much like it had when he'd first arrived, when Kearns had leveled her shotgun at him. Herron hoped that this time, having fired the weapon, she hadn't missed.

He pressed his back against the wall, right next to the door, straining to hear anything inside.

Silence.

As he listened, he peered into the forest to make sure the gunmen hadn't followed him – none had. At least now he was sure he could deal with whatever threat was confronting Kearns without a hostile force hitting him from behind.

Cursing that he'd blocked the hatch, he moved inside. The fire was still bright enough to illuminate the discarded shotgun and the damage where the load of buckshot had torn into the sofa. The lack of a body suggested Kearns had missed, but there was no sign of either her or her target on the ground level.

The trapdoor hadn't been disturbed. That meant they were in the loft.

From his position, he could see nothing amiss up there. He ascended the ladder as quietly as he could, keeping one gun trained on the top, ready for any ambush. Moving against an armed foe with a height advantage was one of the most difficult things an operative faced. But despite the risk of attack, none came.

At the top of the ladder, Herron saw why.

Shade was sitting on the bed, his back resting against the wall. Next to him, hands and feet restrained with zip ties and with a gag in her mouth, Kearns looked at Herron with wide eyes. She thrashed and mumbled, but there was nothing she could do to free herself.

Herron raged at himself for being so blinded by his need to protect Kearns.

He'd chased off after the bait without thinking, while the real threat moved in unopposed. He could have played defense, keeping her safe and seeing off the attackers as they breached the house, but in his bloodlust, he'd rampaged through the forest to kill and maim those who'd dared try to hurt the woman he cared about.

"Empty your weapons then put them on the ground," Shade said, his pistol aimed at Kearns, the consequences of refusal as clear as day. "And don't make me ask again."

Herron did as he was told. When the guns were empty, he eased them to the floor, then stood back up and faced Shade with his hands by his side. The whole time, Shade did nothing but grin, while Kearns continued to moan and struggle.

"She put up more of a fight than you did, Mitch," Shade said. "Shotgun, right as I walked through the door. Shame she missed..."

"What do you want?" Herron's voice was filled with barely suppressed rage. "Let her go, and you can kill me any way you like..."

Kearns began to scream and thrash all the harder, causing Shade to laugh. "I don't think your lady friend is too keen on that idea, Mitch."

"You had me beat at the hospital... you've got me beat here..."

"Yeah, I needed to prove I could track down and bag the most wanted man on the entire planet. Once wasn't enough not to be a fluke, so I did it a few times."

"How?" Herron asked, playing for time. If he could engage Shade's immense ego long enough, he might figure a way out of the bind, or a way to keep Kearns safe. "Why?"

Shade shrugged. "By the time I woke up from my coma, the Master was dead, the Enclave was destroyed, and I had been identified as a shadow operative by every intelligence agency on Earth worth the name. I had agents from six different Federal agencies smiling down at me in my hospital bed, all too ready to throw me in a cell for the rest of my life."

"I—"

"I'm NOT FINISHED!" Shade barked, cutting Herron off and pistol-whipping Kearns for good measure. She moaned and lay still, Herron's blood roaring in his ears. "I'd survived, but you'd removed my ability to work. Even if I could have escaped, I'd have been forced to live like you: on the run, eking out an existence, always looking over my shoulder – forgotten and unremarkable."

Herron waited for him to continue. He couldn't risk Erica taking another shot.

"So," Shade went on, "I spent a lot of time in a cell, and a lot of sessions with people asking me a lot of questions, sometimes with a knife or a bat in their hands. My prospects for the future, once you stripped away all the torture and the blood and the vomit, boiled down to this: what could I offer the United States Government?

"I spent a lot of time reflecting and settled on something that would earn my freedom, make me filthy rich, and give me a chance of finding you if you ever popped back onto the radar. It was a win for everyone but you, Mitch, because I've proven my ability now to find any person on Earth in seconds, if I have a relatively recent photograph of them."

"That's the 'why' sorted," Herron said. "Brutal self-interest, as usual…"

"Thank you." Shade gave a slight nod, taking Herron's words as a compliment. "But that brings us to the 'how,' which I'm sure has been bothering you. How has the great Mitch Herron been continually tracked by all those teams of hitters? It's simple, really. Every cell phone in America is now a mobile facial recognition camera I can use to track down anyone I want."

"That's how you found me at the diner. How did you track me here?"

"We caught you on a cell phone camera of one of the diner's patrons. When we got there, the waitress talked and handed over the phone you'd used. It didn't take much to crack it open and find out where you were. For what it's worth, you had the right idea. You and your lady friend don't have cell phones. If you hadn't stopped at the diner, I doubt we would have found you until you emerged from hiding."

Herron's mind raced. He'd not even considered the phones of other diners as a threat. Via Shade, the American intelligence community now had the ability to turn every cell phone in the country into a surveillance camera. Herron was an expert at living on the run, keeping a low profile, and evading the authorities, but that only worked in a world that was predictable. Cameras could be seen and evaded, humans could be tricked, and cash allowed a measure of anonymity. In a world where everything left an electronic thumbprint and every phone gave the authorities another set of eyes, he wasn't sure he could hide and survive.

Nowhere in the world would be safe for him.

"You know the cool thing?" Shade smirked. "The Enclave was already working on the technology when you put them all through the mulcher. Only the Alphas and the Master knew of the labs and their locations, so when you wiped out everyone except me, it left a lot of technicians working aimlessly for months. They did it because they were afraid of the consequences if they absconded, but when I woke up, there were a bunch of fun things I had access to.

"A quick chat to my new friends in American intelligence convinced them of the value, but I only agreed to hand over the technology on a licensed-use basis. They freed me, and now they pay me a pile of money for access to the technology. Given the leap forward it offered them – live, instant, warrantless surveillance of anyone, anywhere – I had some leverage and they agreed to my terms."

"So tracking me down multiple times was proof of concept."

"To the US Government, as well as to whoever else will pay. Keeping the pistol on Kearns, Shade pulled a cell phone out of his pocket, pointed it at Herron, and snapped a picture. "Smile!"

Herron knew the seconds were ticking down on the encounter. Shade had what he needed and would soon exact his ultimate revenge, which would include Kearns' death as well. He had bought time and got answers, but he hadn't found a solution that would get them both out of this. He watched as Shade raised his gun and slowly squeezed the trigger.

Then stopped.

"You know what?" Shade sniffed, as if he'd had an epiphany. "I'm going to let you and your friend live."

"Why?"

"Because I've missed you, Mitch, and I'm not quite done playing with my food. I want to see if you can find me like I found you, so we're going to play a little game. I'm going to take your friend and go into hiding. If you find me in seven days, I'll return her to you, and we'll have our battle. If you don't, I'll put a bullet in her and then come looking for you, and you *know* I can find you."

"I'm not playing your game, Shade."

"Well, either you agree to being restrained and I take your friend here with me, or you both die now."

"No fucking way!" Herron spat the words like venom. "Kill me and let her go."

Shade shifted his aim to Kearns, his finger pulling back on the trigger.

"Wait!"

Shade held fire. "Decision time. I won't ask again."

"Take her," Herron said, because there was no other option to keep Kearns alive. "But I'll find you."

"I'm counting on it. I've proven the technology enough to get my bags of money, but now I want to prove I'm better than you. So you've got seven days. But to add a little extra to the challenge, I'm leaving the facial recognition system going. If you ping it, I'll pass along your location to my American friends, and you'll have shooters on your ass before you know it."

Herron nodded, and Shade reached into his pocket for a set of handcuffs. Under the watchful eye of the Alpha, Herron secured himself to the loft's safety rail, then sat on the floor. In silence, he watched as Shade dragged a still-fighting Kearns to her feet by her hair, sliced the zip ties around her feet, and forced her down the ladder. The whole time, her eyes stayed locked on Herron.

The look of fear in her eyes hurt him more than any wound he'd ever taken.

"I'll find you, Erica," he said. "And I'll kill you, Shade."

6

———

Herron wasted little time getting to work on the handcuffs – as soon as he heard Shade and Kearns exit through the front door, he began inspecting them, hoping against hope that he might find something amiss with the quality of the steel links or the latch.

No luck.

Cursing, he shifted his focus to the wooden railing. It looked as sturdy as the rest of the well-built shack, but offered the only chance he'd have to free himself quickly. He yanked on the bars, so hard that his hands started to ache. They didn't budge. The raw strength in his muscles simply wasn't enough.

He'd need some extra leverage.

Climbing to his feet, he maneuvered the cuffs up to the top of the rail. Then, gripping the barrier's crossbar, he lifted his feet off the ground and pressed them against the vertical slats on either side of the one he was locked to. Finally, in position, he let go of the crossbar, so nothing but the handcuffs held his body weight.

"Come on," Herron said, hoping the bar would snap, but it didn't budge. "Fucking hell."

It was clear he was going to have to put some heft into it – that meant he was going to hurt. Taking a deep breath, he pulled with his hands and braced with his legs. His hands and wrists immediately burned with pain. He didn't dare bend his legs, reducing the force; either the rail would break, or his wrists would.

With Herron screaming from the pain, the wood gave a sickening crack and then broke, sending him flying hard against the wooden floor. Panting, he allowed himself to spend a second on his back to recover, then he groaned and stood up.

That was part of his problem sorted. But while he'd broken free of his prison, he was still cuffed.

After searching the loft and the two side tables for anything that might help free him of the restraint, Herron headed down to ground level. He went through the shelves and drawers, finding nothing useful, before he saw a pile of paperwork on the corner of the kitchen bench with paper clips binding several sheets together.

"Good work, Doc," Herron said. "Death to the paperless office..."

He took a paper clip and sat on the floor next to the fire. Using its light to help him see what he was doing, he bent and twisted the metal until it resembled a makeshift lock pick. His brow furrowed as he went to work on the mechanism, and finally, with a satisfying click, one manacle opened. The other wrist gave him less trouble, and soon the cuffs clattered to the floor.

Herron sighed with relief and rubbed his wrists, which had been scraped raw by his struggles to free himself. While he had no key to the cuffs, he pocketed them anyway, reasoning they might come in handy, then made for the door. He briefly considered just running through the forest after Shade and Kearns, but deep down he knew that would be a mistake. He didn't know which direction they'd gone in and, combined with the density of the forest and the darkness, he'd have a better chance of finding a needle in a haystack.

Instead, he focused on doing what was smart – something he didn't feel he'd done at all since waking up an hour or so earlier. Knowing every second took Shade and Kearns further from him, he spent only a few minutes searching the shack and the bodies of the shooters. He found precious little by way of information, the goons carrying neither cell phones nor identification that would help him locate Shade. He suspected the amateur thugs were just cut-outs, hired purely as expendable decoys.

But while he struck out on clues, he did much better with supplies.

His search turned up an old backpack bearing the logo of the medical school its former owner had attended, and Herron got to work stuffing it with items he'd need to survive over the next seven days on the run. Given he couldn't go into any stores without risking another customer's cellphone camera picking him up, he would have to be entirely self-sufficient.

It changed the mix of what he'd usually take in the pack.

He filled most of the bag with food – all sorts of canned and packaged goods ranging from beans to beef jerky – enough calories to satisfy his needs, if not his wants, for the next week or so. Next, he found two large plastic bottles and filled them with water; not enough for the full amount of time, but he hoped he'd be able to refill them using a garden hose or similar.

Lastly, he took his pick of the weapons available: a pistol belonging to one intruder because it had more ammo than the cop's pistol, and a nasty-looking tactical knife with a serrated blade one of them had been carrying. It wasn't exactly an arsenal, but it was enough to give him a fighting chance for the battles to come.

Satisfied, he zipped up the bag and left the shack.

His plan to take the car and be on his way was foiled when he found Shade had slashed his tires. Forced instead to continue on foot, he walked back toward the road, staying off the track itself in case any of Shade's amateur shooters were still lurking. There was a boom of thunder and heavy rain started to fall. The forest canopy caught most of it, but Herron still found himself and his bag soaked through in minutes.

At the end of the driveway, Herron kept watch from the shadows for a few minutes, making sure nobody was waiting in ambush, but it appeared that the terms Shade had set were real: he had seven days to stay alive, find Kearns, and kill Shade. While he did not know yet where he'd need to go or what he'd need to do to accomplish this, there were a few steps he could take immediately that would help.

For now, he needed a ride.

Hefting his backpack and keeping a few yards parallel to the road he was following, he set off. Time crawled, and he had drained one bottle of water and started on the beef jerky before he finally heard the promising roar of an engine in the darkness. The sound was distant at first, low-powered like a motorbike, snaking its way along the forested roads. But Herron wasn't exactly spoiled for choice – he'd take what he could get.

As the vehicle got closer, the only sound penetrating the silence of the forest, Herron shoved the last of the jerky into his mouth and drew his pistol. Then, he stepped out into the middle of the narrow road. It was one lane either way, so he easily filled the way ahead, holding up his hand, palm facing out, in the universal sign to stop.

If that didn't work, the pistol he had aimed at the approaching bike sure as hell would.

The rider braked to a halt, still gripping the handlebars tight. "What the hell, man?"

"Off," Herron commanded. "I'm not going to hurt you, but I want the bike."

The rider hesitated for a moment, then reluctantly complied. "Please, man..."

Herron cut the rider – who sounded like a kid – off. "I need it more than you. A woman's life is at risk."

"Fuck her," the rider spat, slowly removing his helmet. "*My* life is at risk if you take the bike."

Herron frowned. The man *was* young, with shaggy hair, a leather jacket, and face tattoos. "You patched?"

"Not yet. And this isn't my bike, so if you take it, they're going to ask me to replace it."

"And you're broke."

"I've got a bit of cash, but not enough to replace a bike in a few days."

Herron sighed. It was just his luck that, instead of a straight carjacking, he'd end up with some kid's sob story about the motorcycle gang he was trying to join. A few years ago, when he was a member of the Enclave, he'd have shrugged and left the kid on the side of the road, regardless of the consequences. But now...

"What sort of bikers play rent-a-bike, anyway?" he asked. "Sounds like a bunch of pussies."

"What the fuck would you know, man?"

"Not much, apparently. Okay, empty your pockets and your bag onto the road, and give me your phone and your helmet, then we ride together. Take me where I need to go, and you'll get to keep the bike."

"Got it," the kid responded immediately, relieved despite his looming status as a prisoner.

"Do anything stupid, you get a bullet," Herron added. "I'm not in the mood for any bullshit."

The deal struck, Herron waited as the kid emptied his pockets and the bike's small cargo bags onto the road and stepped back. After a cursory inspection, Herron kicked his weapons – a flick knife and a set of brass knuckles – into the undergrowth, then nodded at the rider to pick up the rest. Once the wannabe gang member had regained his possessions, Herron put the helmet on, and they were away.

They rode back the way he'd come when he was first looking for the shack. Now that Shade was in the business of selling technology to the American intelligence establishment, he would be more likely to have his base in the country's north than the center or the south, given that's where most of the Federal Government was located.

"We're going to need gas soon," the kid shouted from in front of Herron, a while later.

"Pull into the next station you see. And remember, no bullshit."

The rider complied, stopping at a small gas station

another dozen miles down the road. It had two pumps and a small convenience store, but otherwise it was the sort of place time forgot, with peeling stickers and faded signs. You'd find the same thing replicated along every major interstate highway across America, dotting all the way from city to city...

The thought gave Herron an idea.

"Fill it up," Herron said to the rider. "Then go inside and pay."

Herron climbed off the bike and took a few steps back as the kid set to work at the pump. So far, the wannabe biker had done nothing to rouse his suspicions and seemed genuinely committed to doing whatever was necessary to keep his hands on the bike. That gave Herron the main elements his plan needed to succeed: a reliable ride and a reliable stooge.

He pulled the rider's phone from his pocket. He hadn't planned to use it, not wanting to allow the phone's camera to track him, but now he had an important job for the small Samsung device. He took a second to peel a sticker from the helmet and then reapplied it over the phone's camera before handing it back to the kid.

"I want you to dial a friend and say the following words," Herron said, then told the kid what he wanted.

"That's weird, dude," the rider said. "Why do you want my friends to know that?"

"Just do it. And put the call on speaker."

The rider shrugged, dialed a number, and switched the handset so Herron could hear. A second later, someone answered, but the kid spoke first. "Jimmy? It's me..."

Then he said the exact phrase Herron had given him.

"What the fuck you talkin' 'bout?" said the voice on the other end of the line. "You woke me up for that shit?"

Herron took the phone and killed the call. "Now go inside and pay."

He waited by the bike as the kid did so, wondering if the use of a particular name in the message would trigger the reaction he wanted. He had used it when he had first met Zoe, a British MI5 agent he had helped in Hong Kong and then subsequently relied on himself a few times since. They were allies of convenience, but Herron hoped she would respond to his hail.

He also hoped nobody else in the global intelligence community had flagged the name. As far as he knew, only Zoe knew the alias he had used to summon her twice before. It was possible the British intelligence operative had shared the information with the other countries now hunting him, but he had little choice but to trust her.

The kid emerged from the store and returned to the bike, a pair of chocolate bars and some water in his hands. Herron took his share, scoffing down the supplies. Anything that saved the meager supplies in his backpack was a good thing, even though it was obvious the kid was trying to butter him up, ready to make a break for it at some point.

"What's your name?" Herron asked, before draining the last of the water from the bottle. "We're going to be together a while, so I may as well know what to call you."

"Zach Bolton," he said. "And just how long are you

going to have me riding down the highway with a gun in my back?"

Until I figure out where I'm going, Herron wanted to say but didn't. "As long as I say."

Bolton gave up and climbed back on the bike. The sun was peeking over the horizon as they set off, their surroundings getting brighter by the minute. As they rode, Herron thought about Kearns, wondering how far Shade had taken her and what he might currently be doing or planning to do to her. It was a horrible thought, made worse because his plan to get her back had no guarantee of success.

They rode for an hour, then Herron forced Bolton to stop at yet another gas station. This time, they didn't bother with fuel, simply repeating the same call as before, dialing one of Bolton's friends and giving the name and their current location. Then, they hit the road, only to stop an hour later and do the whole song and dance all over again.

It became something of a routine, putting dots on the map right along the interstate for anyone intercepting the signal. Herron had to rely on only one person having the cipher to crack the code.

By the time they approached their seventh gas station, Bolton was tiring of the riding and the routine. Anyone, no matter the situation, eventually adjusted to their circumstances, and it appeared the young biker was building the confidence to make a move. He was agitated – fidgety with the handlebars and riding more erratically – and that didn't suit Herron's purposes at all.

When they stopped at the gas station, Herron wasted no time climbing off. Their routine well established, he waited for Bolton to go to the gas pump... except, this time, the biker rounded the bike and started toward Herron. He moved fast, raising his fists as he got closer, hoping to get the jump on his captor before Herron could draw the pistol from his waistband.

It was Bolton's bad luck he was picking a fight with the devil.

Herron had the gun out and aimed before Bolton covered half the distance, the younger man's plan telegraphed by his bearing and his mood, ruined before it could get started. Immediately, the biker raised both hands and took a step back; judging by the crestfallen look on his face, he realized he'd given away the golden ticket as well.

"You knew the terms of our deal," Herron said. "I was inclined to just leave you by the side of the road, but I agreed to do you a favor in return for compliance."

"I screwed up, man," Bolton said, a note of panic in his voice. "I've been riding for hours and there's no end in sight, what did you expect?"

"Tired is better than dead, kid. Get the fuck out of here, right now, and I won't shoot you."

"But my bike..."

"Will be a lesson not to fuck around." Herron's voice was devoid of compassion. "I suggest you keep away from those biker buddies of yours, because I doubt they'll be as forgiving as I am."

Bolton looked like he might protest further, then his shoulders slumped, and he walked away. Herron lowered the pistol and watched him go, unconcerned the kid was any sort of threat. He would have been happy to let Bolton keep his bike once he was done with his little game of gas station hopping, but he wouldn't abide someone breaching a deal made in good faith.

The phone in his pocket rang.

Herron pulled it out and looked at the screen, glad he'd had the foresight to cover up the camera; the caller identification didn't recognize the number. He took a moment to think, then shouted at Bolton.

"You want your bike, get back here. And be quick about it!"

The kid turned, a hopeful look in his eyes, then sprinted back in Herron's direction.

"I'm going to answer it and put it on speaker," Herron said quickly. "If you know them, hang up. If you don't, I'll whisper in your ear what I want you to say."

Bolton nodded, and Herron pressed the button to answer the call.

Bolton spoke before the caller could get a word in. "Hello?"

"Where's Herron?" The voice of the woman on the other end of the line was irritated, but it was Zoe.

Bolton looked at Herron.

Herron nodded.

"He's here," Bolton said.

"Prove it," Zoe said.

After Herron whispered into his ear, Bolton relayed the message. "He said Hong Kong was fun and that the hotel was a real highlight."

"Asshole…" There was a decent pause, then she replied. "I'm assuming he can't speak because it's an unsecured line, and doing so would trigger intercepts…"

Bolton looked at Herron, and when Herron nodded, his eyes went wide. He'd just realized that the guy he'd been carting from gas station to gas station along the interstate was someone way more important than a common thief.

"Correct," Bolton finally said.

"Fine," Zoe replied. "Tell him to continue the current travel pattern, and we'll meet you along the route."

"Okay," Bolton said.

Herron killed the call. He'd made contact and Zoe had responded with a plan, so there was no need to talk more. Every wasted second on the call increased the chance of a signals intercept, and he wanted to be on the move again as quickly as possible. But it wouldn't hurt to be extra sure he wasn't being tracked. Cocking his arm, he threw the phone off into the dirt on the side of the road.

"Hey!" Bolton shouted in protest. "That's mine!"

"The bike or the phone..."

Herron waited for Bolton to protest further, but hearing the discussion with Zoe had caused a change in the young man. Knowing Herron was more than he seemed appeared to put an end to the attitude. Instead, he hopped back on the bike, waited for Herron to climb aboard, and gunned the engine – the perfect little chauffeur.

They continued as usual for two more gas stations; at the third, however, Herron got the definite sense something was off. Unable to put his finger on it, he dismounted, reached around and wrapped his palm around the pistol in the small of his back. Without drawing it, he looked around, even as Bolton, blissfully unaware, topped up the bike with the few bucks' worth of gas they'd burned since the last stop.

Herron glanced inside the gas station to the counter.

Nobody was there.

"Stay here," he said to Bolton, snatching the keys from the ignition and sticking them in his pocket. "And don't do anything stupid."

Drawing the pistol, he headed inside. Nothing immediately seemed amiss, but the total lack of any cars or staff in or around the joint was tripping Herron's internal alarms. But a second after he stepped into the building, those alarms went crazy. He didn't need to see to know someone was waiting for him behind the door.

With lightning speed, he spun, whipped up the pistol, and centered it on the face of his would-be ambusher.

7

If his reactions had been anything less than razor-sharp, he might have fired on instinct. Instead, he lowered the pistol, and spoke. "You could have just waited out front and greeted me with a wave..."

"I needed to be sure it was you," Zoe replied nonchalantly. "I've got a sniper in the scrub alongside the highway with a crosshair on your head right now..."

"Why? I've done nothing to warrant that."

"You think so?" She scoffed. "After we worked together in Hong Kong, you only contact me when you need help. It's not what I'd call rock-solid dependability."

Herron winced. The criticism was fair. They'd worked well together in Hong Kong to disrupt – although ultimately not prevent – China's takeover of the island, but since then he had used her only to bail him out. For a man not used to relying on anyone, it was a big concession, but it appeared she expected more out of their professional partnership... or their friendship.

"I'm sorry," he said. "I've got teams of operatives up my ass, and I figured out how they're locating me..."

"Okay, you're a wanted man," she said. "Why is that my problem?"

"They figured out how to use phone cameras as surveillance devices. They can scan and facially identify anyone, even if the camera isn't in use."

"Bullshit," she said. "Nobody has that technology. If anyone did, it would be the US, and they'd share it with their Five Eyes partners."

"Nobody *had* that technology. But trust me, it has been developed. They used it to track me down twice in two days as a proof of concept. Now that technology is for sale to the highest bidder."

"Who's selling it?"

"Not a guy I'd trust to keep it out of the hands of regimes you don't want to have it..."

It took Zoe a second to digest the revelation: that kind of technology was so game changing that every intelligence organization in the world would do anything to get it. Herron let her chew on the news, because he needed her help to find Shade and Kearns, and convincing her of the value of the technology was the best way to secure that.

"Even if it's true, why do you need me?" Zoe said at last, crossing her arms over her chest. "You're more than capable of jamming a spanner in any machinery."

"It's more that you need me," Herron answered. "Aside from the U.S. Government, I'm the only guy who knows who is developing the technology and where to find it."

"And I'll ask again," Zoe said. "Why do you need me?"

"The same guy with the tech has abducted someone important to me. He's going to kill her in a week if I don't find them and kill him."

"Her..." Zoe said, her voice instantly cold.

"The woman who helped me stop the Omega Strain."

"Right." Zoe still looked skeptical, her feelings for Herron plain and complicating. "There's one thing I don't get."

"What?"

"You're a one-man wrecking ball. I've never seen you cower from anything, but you seem afraid now. Tell me all of it from the start."

Herron had already told her a little about his past, but this time he held nothing back. He told her all about his history with the Enclave and with Shade. He told her everything Shade had told him at the cabin, but especially that the former assassin now had state-of-the-art surveillance technology for sale, and he will sell it to the highest bidder in addition to the American Government.

"Damn," Zoe murmured as she digested what Herron had told her. "Imagine that in the hands of China... Iran... North Korea... Hell, terrorist groups would get a kick out of it, locating anyone they want dead."

"And being able to do it instantly. It's full spectrum surveillance, requiring none of the usual infrastructure and agents, available off-the-shelf for a fee."

"Wait outside," she said. "I'm going to pull out my cell phone and call this in. If you're right, I don't want anyone using me to locate you."

Herron nodded and headed back to where Bolton

had been standing near the bike the whole time. He looked like he wanted to say something, but Herron ignored him – he was too busy worrying about what Zoe's reaction would be. Without her help, he wasn't sure he could access the resources he'd require to find Shade and rescue Kearns.

It took a while for Zoe to emerge from the gas station, her phone now nowhere to be seen. Upon seeing her, Bolton tensed, a little uneasy about the fresh addition to an already insane situation. As far as Herron was concerned, however, the biker was irrelevant now, lucky to be alive and lucky to still be in possession of his bike.

"It's sorted," Zoe said. "Time to ditch the kid."

"I'm not going to kill him."

"Kill me?" Bolton cried. He looked from one of them to the other and took a few steps back. "No, I—"

"He's heard me use your name, he's seen your face. He's seen *my* face, Mitch. He's a security risk."

"Not happening," Herron dug in. The kid had been annoying, but he didn't deserve to die. "Period."

"Fuck your moral compass," Zoe said, exasperated. "You're lucky I'm here at all. Don't blow it over him."

"I only found my moral compass in the last few years, Zoe. It's the reason I helped you in Hong Kong when the easy thing to do would have been to help China take over the island. Or, back here in the States, I could have just walked away instead of fighting near impossible odds to stop China from invading Taiwan."

She exhaled heavily, chastised. "I—"

"And *you* are lucky *I'm* here at all," Herron spat. "I need your help, yes, but I'm also offering you the chance to acquire – or neutralize – a technology that will change intelligence gathering and covert operations forever. So, we either let the kid go and be on our own way, ensuring this small security breach doesn't matter for shit anyway, or you can try to shoot him and deal with the consequences."

"Don't forget I've got a sniper out there," she said.

"Well then, try your luck. Let's see if your sniper can shoot faster than me. Bet your life on it?"

There was a tense standoff for a few seconds. Herron hadn't expected her to greet him with hostility, but he guessed she was getting heat from her bosses – she had spent a lot of time and energy helping him, with a negligible return for the British Government. But the reason she was here at all was the promise of the technology he could provide access to... if they helped him.

And, for that reason, he stood his ground.

Eventually, she broke the silence. "My bosses want their own demonstration of this technology before they'll lift a finger to help you. Given the stakes involved in attempting to acquire the technology – pissing off the U.S. Government, for starters – they want to be sure it's worth it. That point, unlike killing your buddy over there, is non-negotiable."

Herron looked at Bolton and jerked his thumb toward the road. "Get out of here, kid. Take the bike and keep your mouth shut. You'd better believe she'll find you if you don't."

He tossed the keys to the bike underhanded to Bolton, who caught them and then wasted no time mounting his steed and roaring away at top speed. As he watched him go, Herron doubted Bolton would say anything to his biker pals or anyone else about his extracurricular excursion, but even if he did, it was unlikely they'd believe him.

"So what's the play?" he said.

"We set up in a location of our choice, flash your face on a phone, and then wait."

"Until a hit team comes swinging for my head?" Herron said. "You're using me as bait?"

"I'm using us as bait, but my orders are to keep you alive, so I'm on the firing line too."

Herron found that slightly surprising, but he'd take the help. He wasn't sure he could take down the next team of shooters on his own. By his count, this would be his fourth such encounter in a couple of days, and he was already hurting. He'd seen Zoe in action and knew she could handle herself, and adding a sniper team would be an extra boon.

"Can you fix me up with some gear before you stick me on a hook and dangle me in the water?"

"Sure."

"And after I prove to you the technology exists?"

"Then I help you find Shade and your friend."

* * *

HERRON HAD EXPECTED they'd go somewhere else to set up their ambush, but Zoe decided they'd make their stand at the same gas station where she'd met him. It had certain advantages – it was remote, it was empty because the owner had already been detained and shuffled away by a British support crew, and they were already there – but Herron would have preferred somewhere offering an escape route if things went bad.

But it wasn't like he had a choice in the matter.

Zoe ordered one of her men to drive the van that had transported them there into the gas station, then she and Herron geared up. They helped themselves to body armor and suppressed submachine guns from the back of the van, everything they'd need to beat the team of hitters who'd be zooming down the highway once the bait was set.

When they were ready, Zoe revealed Herron's face to the camera of Bolton's phone, and they settled in.

Seated on the floor behind the gas station's counter, his gun on the floor next to him, Herron ate one of the gas station's pre-packaged sandwiches while he waited. He justified stealing it by telling himself the food would go to waste otherwise – they'd turned off the gas pumps and signs to make the place look like it was closed. When the shootout came, they didn't want any civilians for company.

Zoe was lurking somewhere, along with her sniper team still concealed with a view of the front of the gas station and the pump area. Time crawled by, and Herron moved onto his third sandwich with no sign of any enemy teams. By now it was the dead of night. Occasionally, a car would pass along the interstate, arousing their interest for a moment, but there was no sign of any shooters.

"Slow going," Zoe said, breaking cover for a moment to liberate a bottle of soda from the gas station fridge. "You better not be bullshitting me."

"I'm wasting my time as well as yours, remember?" Herron replied. "I've only got seven days to find Shade, so I'd rather not be sitting on my ass eating sandwiches."

"That's fair," she said, a little more conciliatory now.

The hours of waiting had given her time to cool off after their confrontation. "Are they any good though?"

"Fine," Herron answered brusquely. He wasn't quite ready to forgive her for being such an asshole earlier, despite needing her help.

"Look, we're going to need to work together to fend off whoever comes looking for you."

"I'm not the one with the attitude," he said, in between bites of his sandwich. "I called you for help, offered you a great opportunity to procure ground-breaking technology in return—"

"I know," she cut in, holding up a hand. "I guess I was a little put out by the fact that you're chasing so hard after a woman."

That confirmed it.

"Look, I don't even know your last name..." he let the sentence trail off, the meaning in it obvious. "Hong Kong was a lot of fun, and I appreciate your help since, but you and I can never happen."

"Why not?"

"You work for the British Government's intelligence apparatus. Most of the rest of the world's governments want me dead. It'd be career suicide for you."

"I know. But I can't help how I feel."

"We don't get the luxury of feelings in our business."

"You seem to have managed it."

"Only after a lot of years. And at substantial cost."

Zoe's eyes widened, and she held up a finger to stop him. She listened for a moment, someone updating her on the tactical earpiece she wore. Pressing the 'talk' button on the device, she said simply, "Distance?"

"What's up?" Herron asked.

"Van incoming, one mile, lights out," she said.

"Showtime."

"Looks like."

They both sprang into action, abandoning their conversation. Herron tossed his sandwich to the ground, picked up his submachine gun, and positioned himself behind the counter. As he did, Zoe jogged out the front door, taking a covered position by the van her team had parked outside. Their plan was to get any new arrivals in a crossfire: Herron and Zoe on one side and the snipers on the other.

He felt confident they'd have the number of any team of shooters that showed up. Concealed, well-armed, and patient, they waited while the suspicious van pulled in and stopped at one of the pumps. The bank of security monitors behind the counter gave Herron real-time footage from the cameras outside, while Zoe was being kept updated by the sniper team.

On the screen, only the driver was visible in the van. He climbed out and walked around to a pump. As he stuck the nozzle into the tank, his head swiveled, looking all around. It was the first sign he might be conducting reconnaissance.

The second was the persistent beeping that started behind the counter where Herron crouched: a signal that one of the gas pumps was ready for use. For the van driver to put fuel into his van, the gas station cashier would need to press a button to release the pump lock.

With no attendant to authorize the sale, no gas would flow down the nozzle when the driver squeezed its trigger, yet the man wasn't getting agitated or giving up.

"It's them," Herron said to himself, knowing nobody else could hear him. If he had comms with Zoe and the sniper team, he could order them to cut the guy down, then fill the van full of lead.

But since he couldn't, he did the next best thing.

He reached up for a headset resting on the counter, which allowed the cashier to speak over the loudspeaker outside. Normally, it'd be used to shoo off loitering teenagers or warn a motorist thinking of driving off without paying. In this case, Herron was going to use it to rain death down on the van driver.

"Contact!" Herron said into the microphone, his words booming over the loudspeaker.

Instantly, his suspicions were confirmed, as the motorist reached around to the small of his back and drew a pistol. It was halfway clear when he dropped, his head split like a melon, the crack of the sniper rifle coming a split-second later.

Silence descended on the scene as the rifle's report faded. Then all hell broke loose.

The back doors of the van opened, and five shooters leapt out. Unlike the driver of the van, there was nothing subtle about their gear: each was dressed in full black tactical gear, minus helmets, and carrying submachine guns.

Herron, Zoe, and the snipers opened fire immediately, ripping into the squad and cutting several down before they could find any sort of cover. The rest returned fire to the only place they could be sure there was a hostile: the place where the announcement that started the firefight had originated.

Herron ducked as shots pounded into the wall and counter, glass raining down on him, but no bullets finding their mark. He took the time to reload, then crawled along the floor, out of the cashier's booth, and into the customer area to find a new firing position.

As he moved, the gunfight outside continued. While he couldn't see it, everything favored the home team. The van team had been caught in an ambush by a prepared force. Caught in the crossfire, they had no position that offered shelter from all shooters. Zoe and her team, meanwhile, had good cover.

Herron made his way to the ice-cream freezer, which stood against the floor-to-ceiling glass overlooking the pump area; the bulky appliance had a decent chance of stopping an incoming bullet and was the best cover on offer. By the time he got there, only one operative was still standing, and he was focused on the incoming fire from the road.

Herron rose from behind cover and fired.

Once. Twice. Three times.

His rounds finished the job, drilling the last enemy twice in the body and once in the head for a final flourish. The hitman dropped, and the gunfire ceased immediately. Both Herron and Zoe stayed behind cover for a few moments, to be sure there were no more surprises, then emerged from cover and headed for the van.

They didn't make eye contact as they moved in, both well-drilled in keeping their eyes on the target. Herron spent a few seconds putting a bullet into the head of each of the shooters, making sure they were neutralized, even as Zoe moved to the back of the van to make sure it was empty. Moments later, both jobs complete, they looked at each other and nodded.

The job was done.

"Who were those guys?" Zoe said, looking down at

the corpses that now littered the forecourt. "Didn't exactly set the world on fire."

"Not a tier one team, that's for damn sure." Herron leaned down and started searching the pockets of one corpse. "No ID."

"We should clean this up, then get the hell out of here," Zoe said.

They spent five minutes dragging the corpses into the back of the van, then Herron slammed the door shut. With the vehicle secured, he got behind the wheel, drove the van across the highway and into a ditch, then climbed out. A few seconds later, he had stuffed a strip of clothing from one corpse into the gas tank and was striking a cigarette lighter he'd sourced from the gas station to light it.

As he crossed back over the highway, the van exploded.

By the time he got back, Zoe was using a hose to wash the blood off the gas station's forecourt, a quick but good enough cleaning job. He fixed her with a gaze. "Happy now? I told you they'd come."

"I'm convinced you're telling the truth," she said. "Now we just need to convince my bosses."

She turned and walked away, already with her cell phone in her hand. While Zoe handled her bosses, Herron grabbed a plastic bag from behind the cashier's counter and started filling it with supplies. He didn't know how long he might have to go before he could restock again with food and hygiene products. What mattered, though, was that he'd secured help to find Shade.

Now he had to wait and see what came next.

8

———————

Herron put his elbows on the hardwood table and stared into space as the MI6 suits at the British Embassy in DC – plus a few on video link – spun themselves in circles trying to come up with a way to find Shade.

"He won't be on any file you have currently," he said, for what felt like the millionth time. "He was an Alpha-level operative for the Enclave, who eluded all of you in this room for years. I pushed him off a roof, and he was immediately scooped up by American intelligence assets and imprisoned. In return for his freedom and a lot of money, he is now prepared to hand the tech over to the Americans."

"Which again begs the question," said one suit, who Herron had taken to calling Pompous Bastard in his head. "If the Americans will get it, why don't we just wait until they share it with us?"

Herron sighed. Pompous Bastard, like most of the others here, was missing the point. Since traveling from the gas station with Zoe and her sniper team, he'd spent several days locked in meetings at the British Embassy. Everyone had been very careful to keep their phones out of any room he was in, to avoid triggering an identification by Shade's tech, but at this point he'd almost prefer a shootout to more talking.

"The United States might give you access to the technology or they might not," Herron conceded. "But as I've been trying to tell you for the last two days, the real threat is that Shade sells the technology to some other regime. Imagine North Korea or Iran or China being able to find anyone they like, using billions of cell phone cameras, then routing assets to capture or kill that person."

Pompous Bastard snorted. "The United States won't let that happen. They'll buy the technology and then keep Shade from selling it on."

"If you think anyone can stop Shade from doing anything, you're sorely mistaken," Herron said. "He's the most capable and ruthless foe I've ever encountered. More importantly than that, he's a survivor."

Herron's words seemed to weigh heavily on his audience because none of them spoke for a few moments. Along with Herron, Zoe, and Pompous Bastard, there were a half-dozen other men and women present either in person or virtually, all with soft hands and expensive clothing. None of them had been in the field, yet they were about to decide the path Herron would have to take to get Kearns back.

A path that would either include the support of the British Government or see him walking away alone.

"We'll need a minute to discuss our options, Mr. Herron," Pompous Bastard finally said. "You can wait outside, and we'll call you in when we're ready."

Herron nodded, made his way to the door. When he was halfway there, he turned. "This is the best chance you'll get to eradicate a weed at the root. If you fail to take it, you'll soon be overrun, and you'll wonder why you ever turned your back on the opportunity. I'll do the dirty work, but I just need some help to get close enough to pull the trigger."

Receiving blank stares in return, even from Zoe, he continued through the door and into the hallway. There was no shortage of chairs, even so, Herron paced instead of sitting. He'd thought contacting Zoe and then demonstrating the technology Shade had at his disposal would be enough to secure the British Government's help, but instead all he'd got was hesitation.

He waited for what felt like an eternity, his pessimism growing. If he had to find Shade and Kearns alone, he'd be starting from square one, having wasted several days. It was time he wished now he could have back.

Eventually, the door opened and Zoe stuck her head out, a thin smile on her face – a surprising change of mood after the coldness she'd back at the gas station. Without speaking, she gestured for Herron to follow her inside.

He did so and closed the door behind him, feeling like he was going to the principal's office or to the biggest job interview of his life. But the atmosphere was a little lighter than before, a little more welcoming as he took his seat again and waited for the verdict the group had reached.

"We'll help you track down this 'Shade' and the woman he's abducted," Pompous Bastard said. "In return, you'll secure the technology he plans to provide to the United States and anyone else willing to pay for it."

"Got it." Herron smiled, the relief on his face obvious. "I—"

"I'm not finished," Pompous Bastard cut in. "Our primary concern – and the reason our deliberations took so long – is your history for biting the hand that feeds you. Multiple times now, you've worked for a person, organization, or government and then burned them once your own interests were served. I'm not interested in your explanations or your denials because this group considers that statement to be a fact."

"Okay…"

"Simply put, we'll work with you in good faith. However, any breach of that faith, and we will spare no expense in hunting down both you and Erica Kearns. Essentially, her life, if you can get her back from Shade, is contingent on your continued good behavior," Pompous Bastard paused, waiting for blowback. When none came, he continued. "This isn't a negotiation. Our offer is take-it-or-leave-it."

Herron hadn't expected such a good deal. Once his greatest enemy was dead and the woman he loved was safe, he'd consider anything else a bonus. Any life, any future with Kearns, any further chance at redemption would all be on borrowed time. He was at peace with that, but he didn't want them to see how eager he was to accept the deal.

Taking a moment as if to consider, he said, "I agree. But if you can't locate Shade, you'll have failed to keep your end of the bargain, and all bets are off."

Pompous Bastard looked at a few of the other suits, who nodded, then back to Herron. "You've got yourself a deal. We find him and help you get to him. You kill him and get the tech. Your friend lives."

"Easy, right?"

"You'll work with Zoe on the details. She has the full support of this group, including the power to terminate our involvement or terminate you and Kearns if she feels you're not living up to your side."

With that, as if some sort of silent command had been given, every one of the suits rose to their feet and headed for the exit, or otherwise terminated their video link. Herron and Zoe both remained seated – he needed to know what came next, and now she was in charge she'd need to brief him. Any initiative Herron had enjoyed even moments ago had been surrendered to secure the help he needed.

"Let's get to it," Zoe said, as if nothing had happened between the two of them. "Before we can find Shade, I need to know what he looks like."

"He looks like the most average, middle-aged, white male you can imagine. But beneath the bland exterior, he is a ruthless motherfucker."

Zoe closed her eyes and massaged her temples. "You're going to need to give me more than that."

"What do you need?"

"A face or a proper name."

Herron had neither. Instead, he rattled off the half-dozen locations he and Shade had encountered one another, and the rough times and dates of the encounters, thankful for his excellent memory to help him dredge up the details. Zoe typed furiously on her laptop, taking copious notes, and when she'd extracted everything from him, she stood up.

"It's a start," she said. "Wait here."

Taking her laptop with her, she left the room. As soon as the door was closed, Herron heard it lock.

"Nothing quite like British hospitality," he muttered.

* * *

"We've had a team working through the night on this," Zoe informed him, a dozen hours later. "They've reviewed footage of the locations you specified, cross-checking with your arrival and departure at each location. You're good, by the way, but you were still caught on some cameras, and we think we've caught you and Shade fighting in three instances – at the hospital, at the shopping center, and on the rooftop."

"The rooftop I pushed him off?" Herron remarked, his tone light. He was impressed with how quickly Zoe's team had navigated the search. "So what now?"

"Now, if you can confirm it's him, we put his identity through every channel we have – HUMINT, SIGINT, the lot – and hope we get a hit. We've never thrown this many resources at finding one target, and we'll have to burn a few assets doing it, but I've been told to hold nothing back given the high stakes of this one. We're basically all in trying to help you on this, Mitch."

While that was reassuring, however, Herron was all too aware of the clock ticking. He'd already wasted around three days convincing the British to help him find Shade, now more minutes or hours or days would be spent waiting idle as they did so. On the flip side, there was no way he'd get any faster results solo, so he went along with the process.

"Sounds good," he said, finally. He stood, rounded the table, and looked over Zoe's shoulder at the photographs on the screen of her laptop. "That's Shade all right."

"You're sure? If we commit to finding the wrong target, the shit that will land on me will be something spectacular."

Herron almost laughed at her fear of the institutional fallout. Instead, he simply nodded. "It's him. I'm one hundred percent sure."

"Okay," she said, shifting to a different browser and typing into some sort of chat program, connecting her to the other British specialists. When she was done typing, she sent the message with an aggressive bash on the enter key. "It's done. It shouldn't take long for someone or some system to find him now that we've got a target lock, then we'll figure out how to proceed."

This time, Zoe didn't leave the room, staying put to get on with her work, answering emails, and doing all the other things a career agent in MI6 did during their normal workday. She sat there for hours, staring at the screen, typing and mostly ignoring Herron. Occasionally, she'd pop her head up to look at him and tell him there was no update, but that was all.

For Herron's part, he had no such distraction: no other work and no other purpose. He was forced to wait in his chair, one of the deadliest operatives on Earth forced to rely on others to locate his target. It was something he'd dealt with earlier in his career, working for the United States military and then the Enclave, but he'd never gotten used to the stasis.

A few times, he got up and paced the room.

A few times, he napped, exhausted from the week or so he'd spent dodging hit teams.

A few times, he just sat and stared at the wall.

At last, it all became unbearable. Herron's leg started to twitch, a sure-fire sign he was just about done with the waiting game. He felt hopeless, a finely honed weapon restricted to a building filled with bright halogen lights and middle-class office workers. It was his idea of hell.

Inertia.

Even harder was reconciling the questions in his head. What if the British, for all their capabilities, never found Shade? What if Shade had been lying and was mistreating Kearns this very second? Could he do better alone, as he had for so many years since leaving the Enclave? Could he trust Zoe, given her obvious feelings for him?

"We found him," she gasped, interrupting Herron's self-interrogation, her face ashen. "And he's close."

Herron sat up sharply in his seat. "Where?"

"New York."

"The places with more people and cellphones per square mile than just about any other place on Earth."

When Zoe nodded, Herron winced at the thought. He'd assumed Shade would try to take Kearns somewhere out of the way, killing her after a week and then using his technology – once again – to find and then ultimately eliminate Herron. Instead, his nemesis had shown up in a place where he'd be easy to find but hard to get to.

Zoe turned the screen so Herron could see it. "He's holed up in a midtown medium-rise apartment block. We got a video hit from a traffic camera on the corner where the building is located, then worked back from there and confirmed multiple sighting on multiple days over the past week."

"Okay."

"There's more. Before they contacted me, by team did some more digging, and it looks like the building has been condemned by the city. Yet Shade has holed up inside with a pack of his goons and all sorts of clearly visible cameras and alarms..."

"If it's the same crew he had used in the forest, they won't be much use."

"Quantity has its own quality, I'm afraid, and there are lots of these guys," Zoe replied. "But I'd be more worried about the cameras and the phones on the street. If he spots you coming, Shade can just point all those goons at you and blaze away. Not even you can dodge that many bullets."

They spent a while working on the problem, Herron finally feeling useful, able to contribute and plan. He worked mostly with Zoe, although other British intelligence staff entered the room or dialed in periodically. Slowly, they pieced together the best picture they could of the building, personnel, and situation Herron would be dealing with.

They were sure the building was otherwise abandoned: the City had condemned it and developers had purchased the site, but until the time came for demolition Shade had set up inside. Either he or the U.S. intelligence apparatus had paid off someone to turn a blind eye to the unusual occupation of the building, and he now had a hideout with defenses that would be difficult to navigate.

The first line of defense was the substantial foot traffic around the building, which meant plenty of phone cameras. Effectively, Shade could use his facial recognition technology as a surveillance net. The second line was the cameras on the building itself. By Herron's estimation, they covered the entire street frontage, as well as the neighboring buildings.

Next up was the shooters. Herron and Zoe had flown a small drone around the building, and had easily spotted several guards, all of whom had handguns. There were at least four on duty at any time. And that was just the protection they could see. Inside the building – if he could make it that far – Herron expected to find more gunmen, more heavily armed.

And that wasn't to mention Shade himself, who had bested Herron on no fewer than three occasions.

In totality, it would see Herron charging right at a highly informed, heavily armed enemy while enjoying none of the advantages he usually relied on: firepower, intelligence, positioning, and surprise. Unlike the past few hours, however, when he'd been fretting and impatient because he had nothing to do but wait, he was energized by the prospect of action. With the problem now clear, he could put his mind to a solution.

And it was a doozy.

"We can take down the cell phone networks of Verizon and T-Mobile nationwide," Zoe said, sometime later. "It's a one-shot weapon using a Trojan we've had in place for a long time."

Herron's eyes widened at the ramifications of what Zoe was suggesting. Such high-level disruption to the cell service of most Americans would light up the threat board of American counterintelligence. It was a huge risk for Britain to take, and a major asset for them to burn. MI6 would have to have a very good plan in place to frame another actor or rogue state for the attack if that trigger was ever pulled.

Thankfully, that wasn't his concern. "How long will that buy me?"

"Not as long as you'd think. We'll knock millions of users off the networks all at once, but as soon as our exploit is found, they'll patch the problem quickly. No more than an hour."

"And it doesn't solve the problem with the traditional surveillance cameras."

"No, it doesn't," Zoe agreed. "And that's one I can't help you out with directly. We've got no technical kill available to us, and my bosses won't authorize direct strikes by British assets on the power grid."

Her statement was heavy with suggestion, leading Herron like a horse to water. He needed no encouragement to drink. "You want me to take out the New York City power grid?"

"That's up to you," she replied in a neutral tone. "But if you want those security cameras and any internal building security disabled..."

Herron looked at her, the ghost of a smile on his face. "When do we get started?"

9

———

"You're five minutes from your target," Zoe's voice crackled through Herron's earpiece as he drove to his target. "As soon as you hit it, you're committed and there's no turning back. You sure you want this?"

"I'm sure," Herron replied, the earpiece's built-in mic relaying his message back to her. "I'll deliver my end of the bargain, just make sure you guys do as well."

There was no response, so he took a left onto the street where his target was located. At two in the morning, there wasn't much traffic around – a necessary countermeasure against Shade's technology. A facial recognition network using every operational cell phone would work exceptionally well during the day in a city like New York. But in the industrial heart of Queens in the early hours of the morning, not so much.

This was the first of four stops he'd have to make, taking down the power grid in New York while the British hackers simultaneously shut down the cell network, rendering Shade's hideout vulnerable. British engineers and grid experts in the employ of MI6 had spent hours working on the problem, informed by an asset in the United States Department of Energy.

Ultimately, they'd developed a risky but workable plan Herron could execute within an hour.

The plan was relatively simple in concept. The experts had identified three electrical substations that were critical for supplying the city. By taking them down, Herron should be able to create a series of cascading failures, affecting redundancy in the system and making it nearly certain he could squeeze the supply to the one building he cared about, at least long enough to complete his real mission.

Herron was drawn to the plan because of the ease of execution, a critical factor given he had very little time left to find Shade and Kearns. While power stations themselves had been hardened in the wake of September 11, there were too many substations and too little budget to defend the entire network. Most were defended by little more than a fence and a lock on a door, and had few or no staff on site most days.

They were ripe for the picking.

As he attacked and destroyed the first, technicians would respond to the incident and work to repair the building itself, while engineers in front of consoles would attempt to reroute the power through other functioning substations. However, if he could hit the three substations in short order, the eggheads said he'd have a two-hour window to get to Shade, with a one-hour overlap of the cell network disruption.

The first target on his list was a massive complex, by far the largest one Herron was scheduled to hit. It was surrounded by a chain-link fence that extended for a hundred feet in all directions, topped with razor wire to keep intruders out. A large sign at the entrance warned of the dangers of high voltage and that only authorized personnel should enter.

Although the main building was unmarked, several large transformers were visible through the fence, and high-voltage power lines that connected to the facility from overhead, stretching off into the distance. The surrounding area, meanwhile, was barren, with no trees or vegetation in sight, as if the electricity channeled from the substation had scorched the earth around it. The only sound was the hum of the transformers.

Herron pulled his car to a stop outside and killed the engine. He waited and watched for a few minutes. Normally, he'd prefer to do at least a day's worth of recon before hitting a target – any target – yet today he was going to hit four separate locations with barely any preparation. Sure, he'd plotted an approach with Zoe and the British experts, but he hadn't had his own eyes on any of the targets.

After a few minutes, he decided he didn't have to worry. There was nobody around. Unbuckling his seatbelt, he opened the door and climbed out of the car, closing and locking it. He popped the trunk, grabbed the duffle bag he'd stowed there, and, fully equipped for the business in hand, he got to it.

At the chain-link fence, he took one last look around, then unzipped the bag and pulled out some wire cutters. Aware he was probably being captured on camera – and law enforcement or private security was probably being contacted to respond – Herron snipped a large circle in the fence, then kicked out the hole and climbed through it.

Moving faster now, he headed deeper into the substation. He had studied the layout of the facility as best he could from maps and pictures, memorizing every detail of the transformers, circuit breakers, and other equipment he needed to destroy. He'd also been told the place would be deserted at this time of night, but he never took anything for granted and drew his pistol.

He made straight for the door, and, finding it locked, dug inside the bag again for a small charge. He placed it just beneath the door handle, pressed the button to arm it, then retreated far enough to ensure he didn't take any damage himself. It fired a few seconds later, with a flash that destroyed the lock and granted him entry.

The inside of the substation was a labyrinth of massive machinery and tangled cables. It was dimly lit by a few flickering fluorescent lights, the air filled with a constant low hum of electrical energy, and the smell of ozone. The concrete walls were stained with oil and dust, and the floor coated in a layer of grime.

Herron headed for the row of high-voltage transformers in the center of the room. Each was the size of a small car, buzzing with energy, and with cables and wires snaking out like tentacles. Next to them were rows of circuit breakers, switches, and other electrical equipment, all designed to manage the flow of electricity through the system.

A flow he was going to dry up.

Wasting no time, he got to work, careful to avoid touching any live electrical components, and knowing even the slightest mistake could result in a fatal shock. He moved with precision, the success of his mission depending on his ability to disable the equipment.

Quickly, he removed the protective cover from a control panel and started tampering with the wiring inside, working from the instructions given to him by the British engineers. He disabled several safety mechanisms and bypassed the circuit breakers, leaving the transformer vulnerable to a catastrophic overload, then repeated the process in several more places.

Next, he moved on to a group of circuit breakers the engineers had tasked him with destroying. They were housed in a row of metal cabinets, but with dozens of such cabinets in the sprawling facility, he had to double-check the number stenciled on the outside. When he was sure he'd found the right one, he quickly opened the doors.

Inside the cabinet, he planted several small explosive charges in a pattern that would ensure maximum damage. When he was done, he closed the door, then did the same in another half-dozen cabinets. The engineers had assured him this would help bring down the power.

After several minutes of meticulous sabotage, Herron was satisfied enough to move on to the next substation. He stuffed his tools back into his bag and was about to move out when he heard footsteps in the distance. He froze, standing as silent as the walls holding up the building, but his heart rate quickened as the footsteps got closer.

He knew that if he was caught now, all his careful planning would be for nothing. He also knew the clock was ticking on the explosives he'd planted; any innocent near them when they blew would be injured or killed, and he couldn't let that happen.

In the shadowy darkness, he peered around the

corner; a security guard was walking towards him, shining his flashlight around the area. He seemed on edge, talking into his lapel-mounted radio, and Herron realized he must have seen the damage to the front door, caused by the breaching charge.

He had one chance to get this right. Waiting until the guard was within arm's reach, he lunged forward, striking the man hard in the temple with the butt of his pistol. The guard crumpled to the ground, and Herron quickly dragged him to the front of the building, far from the blast zone. After securing his wrists and ankles with duct tape, Herron ran, aware that backup would be on the way.

He was outside the fence again when he finally heard the explosions. The damage was done, but Herron couldn't help feeling guilty that he had left the guard to face the consequences. There would soon be an army of people swarming over the joint, and the guard would be asked questions he couldn't answer. Until the next substation went down, anyway.

He left his car behind, walking a few blocks to where British assets had left him another vehicle, one of many he'd be using tonight. Using the same car across multiple targets would make him too easy for law enforcement to spot, because as soon as the reports from the first substation came in, they'd be out looking for the saboteur. He was only a block from his new car when he heard the first sirens.

There was a heap of work left to do, but Herron had never been more motivated.

* * *

"GOOD WORK," Zoe said over the comm after the second substation went down. "One to go."

"Just be ready to knock out the cell network," Herron said. "We need to keep up the pace."

"We'll be ready," she said. "Now get on with it."

The second target had been easier than the first, a smaller brick building on a street corner that didn't even have a fence. All he'd had to do was deal with an old lock on an even older door, giving him access to everything he needed. Three minutes, two charges, one press of a button, and zero security guards later, the place had been dealt with.

It was a ten-minute drive to Brooklyn from where he'd picked up his third clean vehicle of the day. The final substation had a view of Manhattan, so once the facility was destroyed, he'd easily be able to see if the lights on the island had gone out. He was beginning to think he had a shot at this, at least until his self-congratulation was interrupted by blue and red flashing lights in his rear-view mirror, then a siren.

Herron checked his speed, confirming he was five below the limit. "What the hell do you want, asshole?"

If he didn't stop, the cop would bring down hell on him: one or two cops in a squad car he could deal with, but a bunch could be a problem. With a sigh and a crushing sense of the inevitable, Herron pulled the car over, leaving the engine running in case an opportunity to bail presented itself.

The cop took his time emerging from the car, burning precious seconds Herron didn't have. The plan to crash the power grid relied on knocking the substations out fast, before one of the damaged facilities could be repaired.

A single police officer approached Herron's side of the car. Not wanting to antagonize him, Herron wound down the window and smiled when the cop was within earshot. "Evening, officer."

"Could you turn off the ignition, please, sir?" The cop's voice was the perfectly distilled sound of neutrality. He waited for Herron to comply before asking, "Any idea why I've pulled you over, sir?"

"Can't say I do," Herron said, trying hard to hide his annoyance. "Happy to help iron out any problems, though."

"Was that a threat, sir?" The cop took a step back and put his hand on the grip of his holstered pistol. "I'd think long and hard about what comes out of your mouth next."

Herron took a quiet breath, trying very hard not to sigh or say something smart. The cop was clearly looking for trouble, and he'd pulled over the only car on the road trying to find it. His own pistol was jammed into the small of his back, but even sitting at the wheel with a seatbelt across his lap, he was confident he could draw before the cop. He hoped he wouldn't have to waste the time.

"No threat and no problem, officer," he said at last. "I'm just on my way to work. I'd be very pleased to help you with anything you need, then be on my way."

"We'll see about that," the cop mumbled, as if he was unhappy Herron hadn't taken the bait. "I'll need your license and registration. I suspect you may be driving under the influence."

Now Herron did sigh because that was a problem. He had neither a license nor registration, a fact that would escalate the situation whether he liked it or not.

Generally, he hated the idea of harming civilians or law enforcement officers simply doing their jobs, but he was on the clock. If he didn't get to the last substation in time, his only shot to get to Kearns would be blown.

"Let me get those for you. The registration papers are in the glove compartment, and my license is in my wallet, which is in my back pocket," Herron said.

The cop frowned, aware Herron was speaking for the benefit of his body camera, in case he tried to blow him away, then claim he'd been reaching for a weapon. Eventually, he nodded. "Fine."

Except Herron *was* reaching for a weapon.

"I'll get my license first," Herron said, taking his hands off the wheel and reaching around to his back, where the pistol rested. But as he prepared to draw it, the cop's cell phone rang.

"Goddamn it," the officer snarled, as the ringtone – the song *Maneater* – filled the street. He pulled out the phone, then, before answering it, glared at Herron, "Stay right there, hands on the wheel."

Herron nodded and returned his hands to the wheel. He didn't need a shootout if he could avoid one, and maybe talking to whoever was calling – his wife, the maneater? – would put the cop in a better mood. He sat, quiet and still, listening as the cop put the phone to his ear and spoke into it. From the one side of the conversation Herron could hear, it wasn't likely to be a call that improved anyone's mood.

"What? That's bullshit... She's a friend, damn it... Yeah? Yeah? Well, fuck you too!"

Then hung up.

"Fucking bitch," the cop sighed.

"Sounds familiar," Herron said, trying a new tack to sail through this situation. "Left my wife a year ago."

"Cheated?" The cop's voice softened a little as he lowered the phone to his side...

... and the camera tracked across Herron.

"Sorry you're in a similar boat," Herron said. His image from the phone would be speeding through the ether; he had maybe minutes until his presence was spotted by Shade's people. "What did you need again?"

The cop looked at him for a few long seconds, sizing up what he wanted to do, then he shrugged. "Drive on."

And just like that, the cop's attention was elsewhere.

As the officer walked back to his vehicle, Herron's mind raced from gladness that he'd avoided having to draw his gun on the cop, to concern that the phone had picked him up and was now in real danger. At the very least, the hit would mean Shade now knew he was in the city. It was the first real setback of the night, and Herron couldn't afford even one.

Because even one could be deadly.

* * *

HERRON LEANED against a tree and looked out over the Hudson River to the Manhattan skyline, which had just gone dark. He grinned. "Jackpot."

He was hoping against hope that his efforts to take down the grid wouldn't be fleeting and that the engineers had got it right. If the power to Manhattan wasn't back up within twenty minutes, he'd been told, it was unlikely the damage could be fixed tonight. Crews would have to be woken, parts driven around or ordered, fires put out, and repairs made.

He waited twenty-five, but the city remained dark for the whole time. Taking out a few crucial chokepoints in the system meant the whole thing had crumbled. He felt a little sorry for the people whose lives would be disrupted by the citywide blackout, but it was necessary to get Kearns back. He'd do anything necessary to ensure that.

"Power is out," he said over comms. "The whole city has been dark for twenty-five minutes."

"We're watching remotely," Zoe replied. "Give the word, and we'll bring down the cell phone networks."

"Well, we've already kicked out one strut of modern society," Herron said. "Why not two?"

"It'll be done in five minutes," Zoe said. "Get moving, and good hunting."

10

Herron looked down the scope of the sniper rifle. Zoe's people had left it in a hotel room that had a balcony overlooking Shade's condemned building, along with a selection of other guns, gear, night vision goggles, and a Kevlar vest.

He was as ready as he'd ever be.

As expected, the power was still out and now the cell phone network was down too, so he could be far less cautious about showing his face. Surveying his target from the balcony in the dark, he doubted anyone could see him. But through his night-vision scope, the enemy shooters were as clear as day.

Even in the dark, he knew Shade's hideout was eight stories tall. Its windows were boarded up, its paint was peeling, and weeds grew tall in the cracked pavement that surrounded it. Hitting the building a few times with a wrecking ball would improve it, but despite its flaws, it had proven to be an effective bolthole.

In planning the operation, Herron had done some research on the building and its origins, hoping to get some clues about what he might find inside. A century ago, it had been a luxurious residence for the wealthy elite, but as time had marched on it had been abandoned, a forgotten relic of a bygone era.

All that remained was the shell, left to decay and crumble.

A tomb... although for whom, he didn't yet know.

Moving from the architectural to the biological, Herron scoped four guards at the front of the building.. Aside from the front door, there was a guard posted on the fire escape, plus two roving teams of two patrolling in no discernible pattern, walking around the block on the lookout for anything amiss.

It was a formidable layer of defense, even after Herron had stripped away the phones and cameras, but nothing a bit of hard work wouldn't fix. That, and the night vision goggles. Prepared to kick off the deadly game, he took a deep breath and steadied his aim, setting his sights on one of the four guards near the door.

Herron fired.

The round hit the guard in the head. He collapsed, and the other three guards near the door immediately sprang into action, searching for the source of the shot. It was a futile effort in the dark, with the power out, and Herron dropped them with three more shots, his aim flawless.

Instantly, he shifted his aim to the guard on the fire escape, in time to see the man had spotted Herron's position and was raising his weapon.

Both fired at the same time.

The guard's submachine gun was horribly inaccurate over such range, and his shots pitter-pattered harmlessly off concrete, the closest shattering a few windows around Herron.

With his high-end sniper rifle, Herron's shot was perfect. He drilled the guard, who toppled over the railing of the fire escape and down to the ground.

In thirty seconds, Herron had annihilated most of the sentries, none having the chance to retaliate in any meaningful way.

Four shots later, he'd dealt with the two roving teams – nine men taken off the board with nine pulls of the trigger.

Herron wasted no time, because every second lost gave Shade more time to prepare or harm Kearns. He tossed the sniper rifle aside, settled his night-vision goggles over his eyes, and picked up the device at his feet: an MI6 prototype that had Herron feeling a little nervous but which offered him the best chance to get inside the building before more guards, or even law enforcement, arrived in force.

It looked like a very small rocket launcher: a four-foot cylindrical metal tube with a grip and a trigger. Putting it to his shoulder, he aimed at the brick wall right above the fire escape he'd just cleared, careful that the rear of the device was pointing at one of the walls behind him rather than a window. After a quick breath, he squeezed the trigger.

The launcher fired a line from either end of its tube with such propulsive force Herron was suddenly curious about how the device worked. Behind him, the cable didn't have far to travel before the clawed head of the line bored into the wall, while the end fired out the front of the launcher flew far over the chasm between the hotel balcony and the target building, embedding in the brickwork.

"Moving in," Herron spoke into his earpiece's inbuilt microphone, then did the last thing he wanted to do.

Gripping the tube that had housed the device, he leapt off the balcony.

Riding the zipline, Herron rushed at breakneck speed toward the derelict building. The wind resistance was like sandpaper on his skin, but as he shot across the gap, Herron found himself grinning with exhilaration.

Judging his landing the best he could, he let go of the device, arms flailing as he dropped like a stone, painfully aware of the unforgiving concrete alleyway below if he got it wrong.

He slammed into the fire escape, instinctively gripping for the railing...

... and catching it...

... only for his momentum to carry him under the level he wanted, to the one below. He crashed into the metal walkway, crying out in pain from the hard landing and the fiery lances of agony in his wounded hand. He rolled onto his back and groaned but didn't allow himself the luxury of even a second to recover.

It was time to finish the job.

He got to his feet, hefted his bag over his shoulder, and drew his pistol before trying the window next to where he'd landed. It was unlocked. He slid it open and climbed through. A flick of a switch turned on the torch attached to his pistol, revealing a dirty, dark apartment that couldn't have been occupied in years.

He swept the room with his pistol and found it empty. Not surprising, since Shade lacked the personnel to cover every room and window inside his makeshift headquarters, relying instead on his cell phone facial recognition, his cameras, and his ground-level goons.

All which Herron had removed.

Now it was time for the kill.

"This is Herron, I'm inside," he said to Zoe over the comm.

"We saw," Zoe's voice said into his ear. "We've got a drone in the air watching. That was... impressive."

"Any new intel about what I'm facing now?"

"We've got a handful of heat signatures."

"Where?

"You're fine to leave the apartment you're in. Turn left, and head to the stairs, then head up two levels. There are four readings in a room there. I think it's where Shade and Kearns are."

"Any other contacts?"

"Not anywhere near you," she said, although her voice didn't have the level of conviction Herron would prefer. "You should have an unimpeded path if you move quickly."

"Copy."

Herron left the apartment, stalking silently down the hallway towards the stairs. He ignored the abandoned rooms on either side of him; their doors were closed, and Zoe had told him there was nobody inside. The drone's heat sensors wouldn't be perfect, but he had to balance that risk against the time it would take to check every room he passed. And Zoe's intel had served him well so far. Whatever her feelings for him, it didn't seem to have caused a problem in her conduct of the mission, which had been as professional and thorough as the other times he'd worked with her.

He took the stairs two at a time, far more aggressive

than usual. He went up one level. Two. Then he burst through the door...

... and was met with withering gunfire.

He cursed and backed back into the safety of the stairwell as rounds pounded into the doorframe and the wall. Thankfully, the building's stairwell was concrete, a fire-safety feature that stopped bullets from punching through drywall and into his flesh. Mouthing a silent thanks to the architects who'd designed the place, he stayed bunkered down while the fury of the enemy shooters raged around him.

"Found those hostiles!" Herron said loudly, so Zoe could hear him over the gunfire. "I'm pinned down!"

"We can see on the drone's thermal cam." Zoe's voice had all the serenity of a woman not getting shot at.

"Hope you're enjoying the show! Got any good news for me?"

"There's only two of them between you and Shade."

"I can work with that," Herron said. "I need you to tell me exactly where those shooters are..."

"One is halfway down the hall – call it thirty yards. The other is closer – fifteen yards or so."

"Cover?"

"Hard to know," Zoe said. "But if I cross-reference the floor plan against the positional information from the drone... I'd guess they're taking cover inside the doors of old apartments and popping out to shoot."

"Thanks, I'll take it from here."

Reaching inside his bag, he felt around until he found what he needed. The British had provided a few more goodies, and the two frag grenades he pulled out would be perfect. Normally, such weapons would be useless in the close confines of an apartment building, due to the risk of civilian casualties. In addition, with the two shooters so close, he would run the risk of getting caught by the shrapnel himself.

Thankfully, the apartment building was unoccupied, and the same concrete stairwell that was protecting him from bullets would also shield against the explosions.

But it was a gamble, because as far as he knew, Shade and Kearns weren't protected by concrete. He was betting on them being far enough away to avoid the shrapnel, but it was a chance he had to take. The grenades were his ticket out of the stairwell.

He pulled the pin and popped the safety clip of each grenade, then chanced the incoming fire enough to toss them out into the corridor. They bounced along the tiled floor, then detonated within a second of each other. The explosions were muffled by the thick walls, but he knew that damage would be devastating.

He hefted the bag onto his back, drew one pistol and then another, and emerged from the stairwell.

Chaos reigned.

The light of the pistol's torch showed the grenades had turned the corridor into a haunting monument to violence. The air was thick with the acrid scent of smoke, and the once pristine drywall was pitted with shrapnel impacts. Debris littered the ground, and the occasional spark flickered from exposed wires. Halfway down the hallway, two small holes in the floorboards marked the spots where the grenades had exploded, and the force of the blasts had blown out a section of a nearby wall.

The grenades had done a whole lot more to the enemy shooters, though. One lay on the ground, unmoving. Further down, another man lay screaming, his clothes torn and bloody from flying metal. Herron fired two shots into the guy's head, silencing him. He wasn't after intelligence, and he wasn't showing any mercy.

He was here for Shade and Kearns. Everyone else could stay out of his way or die.

He slipped down the hallway, both his pistols searching for targets, on the road to what was surely the ultimate showdown of his professional life. He wasn't sure he could beat Shade in a one-on-one fight – in fact, he was pretty sure he couldn't – but he owed it to Kearns, himself, and his own conscience to try.

His nemesis was a monster who needed to be slain, the very picture of evil. It was a picture Herron himself would have resembled, had he not met Kearns. His very first encounter with her had set him on a path of redemption.

It had led him to avert a catastrophe, destroy a clandestine organization that unleashed mayhem for the highest bidder, foil a regime intent on being the 21st Century's worst international player, and – most importantly – make up for some of the evil he himself had committed.

It had restored his humanity.

"Take your next left, then a right, and you'll reach the room they're holed up in," Zoe broadcast into his earpiece. "They haven't moved an inch since you started shooting up the place."

"Okay. Going in for the ki—"

"Wait!" Zoe's voice was panicked now. "A couple of vans just pulled up out front. Reinforcements. Lots of them."

"How many? And how long have I got?"

"At least four... six... fuck, another van," she said. "If they take the stairs, they'll be on you in a few minutes. And now some cops are arriving, too."

"I need some backup!"

"I'm not authorized to lift a finger to help you out of there. You need to bail. Leave him – leave her – or you're fucked."

"Then I guess I'm fucked. Thanks for helping get me this far," Herron said, then reached up to his ear, removed the earpiece, and dropped it on the ground.

Following her last piece of intel, he took the left, then the right, moving as fast as he could and hoping Shade hadn't shifted position to ambush him. Finally, he pressed against the doorframe of the target apartment. Taking a deep breath, he moved through the open door, pistols up to aim at the pair inside.

And then, in the torchlight of both his flashlight and someone else's, he could see them.

Shade sat in a chair, his pistol – with its own torch – aimed at Kearns.

Kearns was seated also, terrified but unharmed, with no visible scars, cuts, or bruises.

The picture of good health.

Except she was wearing a bomb vest.

"Shoot him, Mitch!" Kearns said. "He's got help on the way!"

"I wouldn't," Shade said. "I've got a dead man's switch."

Herron focused on Shade's other hand, on the small black device that could be a detonator. If Herron opened fire, he might be able to take him out before he shot Kearns. But if Shade was holding a dead man's switch, killing him would release his finger from the trigger that was stopping the vest from blowing.

"This wasn't the deal, Shade!" Herron hissed. "You said if I found you, we'd fight, but she'd be safe!"

"That was always your problem, Mitch. You think this game is fair."

"Let her go!"

Shade fired.

Kearns cried out in pain as Shade lunged at Herron.

Herron had him cold in his sights, but didn't fire.

Killing Shade would kill them all, the bomb devastating the whole room.

"Bad luck, Mitch!" Shade sneered as he threw punches at Herron. "Your lady friend is bleeding out, I've got help a minute away with orders to shoot her dead, and you can't do a thing to harm me."

Herron said nothing, using his pistols as hand-to-hand combat weapons, fending off his blows. As they danced their deadly dance, the flashlights on both of their pistols strobed about, turning the abandoned apartment into a macabre disco.

While fighting to avoid Shade's blows, Herron's mind raced to find a way out of the situation, a potentially deadly distraction. But from every angle, it looked like the perfect trap. Shade could do whatever he liked, and he was unable to resist. All he could do was defend, waiting for the inevitable.

"Let's ditch the guns, eh?" Shade grinned, then punched out at Herron's hands.

Herron was so wary of inadvertently triggering the detonator that he let the blows land. They hurt like hell, especially on his wounded hand, and he lost his grip on the weapons, which clattered away and out of reach, although thankfully the torch still provided enough light for him to see.

"Keep playing defense and I'm going to shoot her in the head," Shade said, disappointed. "I want effort."

"Disarm the bomb," Herron grunted between blows. "Then you'll have all the effort you can handle."

"Doesn't work that way, but how about a deal?" Shade said, backing off and circling him in a combat stance. "I'll toss you the switch. It won't trigger if you press down on it in three seconds. Then you've got no reason to hold back. If you beat me, she survives, until the army of shitheads that is on the way arrives, anyway. But if you can't, I kick the shit out of you until you black out or die, then she goes *boom*."

"Great plan," Herron snorted. "If you kill me after I've got the switch, you'll die too."

"You think I'm stupid? That bomb's not big enough to blow me up. It's barely enough to take her down."

With no warning, Shade tossed the switch like a fastball, high over Herron's head.

It was an instant test for Herron's reflexes, a do-or-die moment in which failure would end the life of the woman he'd come here to save. Like a flash, he stretched up to catch the switch. It slapped into his wounded palm, but no amount of pain would stop him from grabbing and squeezing it.

He had maybe a second to spare.

Now, if he fell, it'd be his finger releasing the trigger that would kill her.

He charged forward, launching a flurry of jabs and uppercuts that belonged more in a bar fight than a battle between elite operatives. One blow clipped Shade's jaw, staggering him, but the rest were blocked or dodged. All the while, Herron kept his finger jammed on the trigger protecting Kearns' life.

The pair sized each other up, looking for an opening. Herron feinted with his left, then threw a right cross. Shade blocked it and countered with a kick to Herron's thigh. Herron stumbled but quickly recovered. More rapid strikes and blocks followed, each fighter trying to gain the upper hand.

Herron landed a solid punch to Shade's jaw, but Shade retaliated with a knee to his gut. The breath whooshed out of him, but he didn't give up. With a burst of energy, he seized Shade's arm and twisted it behind his back. Shade cried out in pain but slipped free and elbowed Herron in the face.

He staggered back, blood streaming from his nose, and Shade followed up with one punch to his jaw. Then another. Then another. Each landed like a sledgehammer, each enough to put most people on Earth onto their ass. But it took the full three to do that to Herron.

He dropped to the ground, stunned. It took every bit of energy he had left to keep his finger on the switch, allowing Shade to stay on him, driving kick after kick into his torso and head. Any ability to defend himself was gone, overwhelmed by the precision and brutality of Shade's assault.

"Stop," Herron mumbled, blood filling his mouth and dribbling down his chin. "You win."

Shade delivered another kick to his ribs. "Say it again."

"You win, Shade."

The impacts ceased, and Herron rolled onto his back, staring up at his assailant, his eyes puffed up, and his vision blurry from the punishment he'd taken. The grin on Shade's face was the most haunting thing he had ever seen. Herron knew this was the moment of his death, yet his overriding thought wasn't for himself.

"Leave her be, Shade," Herron said, his voice pleading. "Do what you want to me, but let her go."

"No can do, buddy. You played the game and you lost."

Herron tried to push himself up again, driven by hate and fury for this man, by the love and desperation he felt for Erica. He made it to his hands and knees before Shade delivered another brutal punt to his face, snapping his head to the side, totally disorienting him. He crashed to the ground, and his vision went dark.

When it returned, perhaps a moment later, Shade was no longer standing over him...

... he was beside Kearns, his gun pressed into her skull.

She was bleeding, crying, frantic, and the sight drove Herron to try one more time.

Every bone and joint and muscle in his body ached as he got to his feet. He staggered closer to Shade and Kearns, focusing on the fateful words the former Enclave Alpha had said a few moments before – the only thing that gave Herron and his lover the smallest of chances.

"You'd have to be standing on top of her..." he mumbled.

"What's that?" Shade snorted, then nodded mockingly. "You're right. If you detonate the bomb now, it'll kill me too. But your lady friend will be dead too, so..."

"I know," Herron said, ambling even closer like a

walking corpse. "And she knows, too, Shade. That, I'm sure of."

"Then we're at an impasse," Shade said, clearly not convinced that Herron would blow up the woman he loved to smite his foe, but clearly not convinced he *wouldn't*, either. "So how about I leave you two here and exit stage left, and you agree not to blow me and her to smithereens. Of course, there's a dozen or so dudes on their way, so choose fast."

Herron thought about it for a nanosecond. "Toss me the weapon, then get the hell out of here."

A smirk turned up the corners of Shade's mouth. "You're getting soft, Mitch. It'll be the death of you."

"But not today."

"No, not today."

Shade tossed the pistol underarm to Herron. It sailed through the air, and he caught it with his free hand, bringing it up and settling his aim on Shade, who had already started moving away from Kearns and the potential blast zone.

"Shade," Herron called out.

"Mitch," Shade said, turning to see the pistol aimed at him.

"You know your problem?"

Shade froze, then sighed. "I imagine you're about to tell me."

"You think this game is fair."

Herron fired.

The round bit deep into Shade's shoulder, and Herron shifted aim to the former assassin's stunned face...

... as a flashbang exploded behind him.

Shade's cavalry had arrived.

The detonation was out in the corridor, too far away to do much more than briefly distract Herron, but it was enough. By the time he refocused on Shade, ready to finish the job, his nemesis was gone, having slipped away through the room's other exit.

Herron cursed, then switched to assess the oncoming force. Peering out into the hallway, he saw around a dozen shooters making entry into the space, the flashbang aimed to disorient anyone who might be waiting at the top of the stairs.

He ran over to Kearns and handed her the dead man's switch, wordlessly communicating what he needed her to do – hold on to the trigger no matter what. Pistol in one hand, he used the other to grab her arm, and then they ran, ducking through the same doorway through which Shade had fled.

If it could offer him an escape route, it could do the same for them.

Erica whimpered with each limping step, and Herron glanced at her leg. Shade's bullet had entered her thigh, and while it didn't appear to have severed an artery, there was enough blood to be a concern. Unfortunately, getting clear of the shooters had to come first.

"It's going to be okay, Erica, you're safe now," he said, moving them down the hallway and past apartment after apartment. "We'll get out of here, then get you to a doctor."

"Bullshit, Mitch," she said between tortured breaths, the pain overwhelming. "There must be a dozen armed men on our tail."

"Yeah, but I've got something they don't."

Herron kicked in the door of one of the empty

apartments, dragging her through. He gestured for her to keep going, then dug into his bag, pulling out the last of the supplies inside – a pair of small shaped charges and a detonator. Quickly, he set one on either side of the door, then bolted after her to the kitchen area.

He took cover behind the bench with a view of the door. Pistol in one hand, detonator in the other. A second later, Shade's goons moved inside, showing the same quality and discipline they had displayed at Kearns' forest shack.

Their lack of training and experience was the end of them.

Herron ducked down and blew the charges.

The charges were designed to breach a door and packed more than enough punch to tear apart the doorframe and everyone crowding near it. After the explosions came the screams: multiple men were crying out, but it wasn't enough to make Herron confident the job was done.

It wouldn't be enough – couldn't be enough – against the army of shitheads spewing into the building, but it was all he had left. If he was going to go down, it would be fighting and dying for the woman he loved. But then he had another idea.

"Turn around," he said to Kearns, trying his best to smile reassuringly. "Quickly."

She did so, and Herron inspected the explosive vest Shade had draped over her. Only a zip held it in place, and it was a simple matter to get it off her. Along with the dead man's switch, he now had another makeshift weapon with which to thin out the attackers' numbers.

Attackers who were now on top of him.

Herron grunted as the first gunman round the

counter got the jump on him, firing into his chest. The vest Zoe had left for him saved his life, although the impact of the round at such close range was like being hit by a car, cracking a rib. Desperate, he raised his own pistol and fired, drilling his foe between the eyes.

Grunting in pain, Herron hurled the bomb vest over the bench like he was lobbing a grenade, then nodded at Kearns. She took her finger off the dead man's switch, Herron covered his ears, and silently counted down from three.

It went off with considerably more oomph than the shaped charges. Shade had either been lying or wrong about how much explosive was in the vest, which maybe explained why he'd taken the first backward step ever in multiple encounters with Herron.

As the dust settled, Herron emerged from cover. Moving slower than normal, he put a round into the head of the one shooter still standing, a man so tardy in getting through the door that he'd missed the explosive fun. Then he emptied the rest of his clip into the wounded amateurs, finishing off Shade's army of halfwits.

And just like that, it was over.

Herron took a second to confirm his desperate but determined efforts had wiped out Shade's reinforcements, peering out into the hallway, but it was clear he and Kearns were alone with nothing but the bodies.

Shade was nowhere to be seen.

He put his gun on the ground and dug through the bag, looking for the basic battlefield first aid kit the British had included amongst his supplies for the mission. After finding a dressing, he used his knife to cut away at the clothing around her wound, then ripped the dressing out of its pack and slapped it down on her wound. She cried in pain, but after one firm press, the adhesive stuck to her skin, and would help to prevent more blood loss until Herron could get her some help.

Having done the best he could for her wound, he helped Kearns to her feet, bitter-sweet about how things had played out. Accepting Shade was still alive was a bitter pill to swallow. This was a man who'd been above the grit and the gore Herron was forced to contend with daily – a gilded disciple of the Master and an organization long gone, pining for a return to the old ways even as he whored himself to the highest bidder. But in foiling his plan, Herron felt he had graduated to Shade's level, even if he hadn't killed him.

It was a small win, but he'd take it.

Slowly, he led Erica back through the devastated building, back to where he had dropped the earpiece that would connect him to Zoe. He had to search for a second, but he eventually found it, reaching up to put it in his ear.

"It's me," he said, finally connected to the comms again. "I got Kearns…"

"About time!" Zoe replied. "We didn't move heaven and Earth helping you just so you could go rogue."

Exhausted, sore, and out of patience, Herron said nothing.

"Did you get Shade?" Zoe's voice was a little calmer now, hopeful despite the friction his abandonment of the earpiece had caused. "And the facial recognition technology?"

"No."

"No what?"

"I traded Kearns' life for Shade's. He got away and I didn't get the tech."

There was a long period of silence, so long Herron almost thought she'd cut the comms.

"Mitch, listen carefully," Zoe said, her voice cold. "As far as we're concerned, nothing has changed. You owe us that technology, regardless of context, and your... friend's life is our insurance policy. I—"

Herron took the earpiece out of his ear and stamped on it.

"What's going on?" Kearns asked, still in pain from the gunshot wound in her thigh. "Mitch?"

"Nothing," he said, wrapping an arm around her. "We're going to get you help, then make up for lost time."

ABOUT THE AUTHOR

Steve P. Vincent is the USA Today Bestselling Author of the Jack Emery and Mitch Herron conspiracy thrillers, and the Frontier Saga science fiction series.

Steve has a degree in political science, a thesis on global terrorism, a decade as a policy advisor and training from the FBI and Australian Army in his conspiracy kit bag.

When he's not writing, Steve enjoys whisky, sports and travel.

You can contact Steve at all the usual places:

stevepvincent.com

steve@stevepvincent.com